A SONG ONLY I CAN HEAR

A SONG ONLY I CAN HEAR

Barry Jonsberg

SIMON & SCHUSTER BOOKS FOR YOUNG READERS
New York   London   Toronto   Sydney   New Delhi

SIMON & SCHUSTER BOOKS FOR YOUNG READERS
An imprint of Simon & Schuster Children's Publishing Division
1230 Avenue of the Americas, New York, New York 10020

First published in Australia in 2018 by Allen & Unwin
First US Edition 2020

For information about special discounts for bulk purchases, please contact Simon & Schuster
Special Sales at 1-866-506-1949 or business@simonandschuster.com.
The Simon & Schuster Speakers Bureau can bring authors to your live event.
For more information or to book an event, contact the Simon & Schuster Speakers Bureau
at 1-866-248-3049 or visit our website at www.simonspeakers.com.
Jacket design by Lizzy Bromley
Interior design by Tom Daly
The text for this book was set in Minion Pro.
Manufactured in the United States of America
0320 FFG
2 4 6 8 10 9 7 5 3

Library of Congress Cataloging-in-Publication Data
Names: Jonsberg, Barry, 1951– author.
Title: A song only I can hear / Barry Jonsberg.
Description: First US edition. | New York : Simon & Schuster Books for Young
Readers, 2019. | "First published in Australia by Allen & Unwin in 2018." |
Summary: Thirteen-year-old Rob, a painfully shy wallflower, receives a
series of mysterious text messages challenging him to leave his comfort
zone as he tries to impress new student Destry Camberwick.
Identifiers: LCCN 2018049878| ISBN 9781534442528 (hardcover) | ISBN 9781534442542 (eBook)
Subjects: | CYAC: Bashfulness—Fiction. | Self-confidence—Fiction. |
Grandfathers—Fiction. | Family life—Australia—Fiction. | Gender
identity—Fiction. | Australia—Fiction.
Classification: LCC PZ7.J7426 Son 2019 | DDC [Fic]—dc23
LC record available at https://lccn.loc.gov/2018049878

For

Stephanie Spillett

Lucy Gunner

Ira Racines

You don't love someone for their looks,
their clothes, or their fancy car, but because
they sing a song only you can hear.
Oscar Wilde

PROLOGUE

"MUM," I SAID. "WHEN YOU LOOK AT DAD, DO YOUR
pupils dilate? Is there a rush of blood to your epidermis and
a fluttering in the pit of your stomach?"

Breakfast is the perfect time for serious conversation.
A new day is starting but it's the calm before the day's
metaphorical storm.

Mum looked at Dad.

Descriptive note: father. Name: Alan Patrick Fitzgerald.
Age: . . . who knows such things? Old. Not really old, like
Grandad, who is little more than a collection of wrinkles
in a nest of grayness, but averagely old. Could be forty-five.
Could be fifty-eight. An age, I imagine, when you've stopped
caring how old you are. Or possibly even stopped remem-
bering. Dad, at least when sitting at the kitchen table, is a
sphere on top of a sphere, like a fleshy snowman. His head is
bald and he has more chins than standard. I sometimes get

the urge to put my fingers up his nostrils, such is the resemblance to a bowling ball, although I have resisted this, for obvious reasons. Alan Patrick Fitzgerald also has a belly like a sail in a strong wind. It stretches the fabric of his white shirt to the extent that gaps between buttons gape. Dark and wiry hairs protrude from those gaps as if he keeps either a dark rug or a dead primate tucked down there. Maybe his head hair migrated south.

Mum looked at Dad. Dad looked at the sports pages of our local newspaper, lost in the US Open golf tournament, and deaf to my words. She glanced back at me.

"I don't know about fluttering," she said, "but he sometimes *turns* my stomach."

I gave a small, disapproving frown and cocked my head to one side. Mum buttered toast.

"Why do you ask, Rob?" she said.

"I have become a student of love," I replied. "It's a mystery and I hoped you and Dad could shed some light on it, since you've been together for many, many years. Do you still display all those signs of love?"

Mum chewed her toast and considered the question.

"The thing is," she replied finally, "it's impossible to maintain that first heady flush of love. No one's got the stamina."

I thought about this. If Mum was constantly blushing, with pupils dilating and stomach fluttering, it would be difficult to carry on a normal daily routine. You'd bump into things, for example, and be permanently orange, like Donald Trump.

"So love fades. Is that what you're saying?"

"No. 'Fades' isn't the right word. It changes." She gazed at the dining table as if for inspiration. Or maybe it was just to avoid my eyes. Some people, according to reading I've done on the subject, find the topic of love embarrassing, if not distasteful. Then she *did* meet my eyes, as though a decision had been made. "You're probably old enough to talk about this kind of stuff," she said. "And maybe it's time we did. The thing is, all those things you described—the rush of blood, the eyes dilating, the butterflies in the stomach—well, those are more to do with *physical* love, with desire. Do you know what I mean?"

I looked at Dad and tried to imagine someone finding him physically attractive. I couldn't, but that didn't mean it was impossible.

"Sure," I said.

"Proper love is more than that," she continued. "It's to do with trust and affection and knowing what the other person is thinking without being told. It's to do with the ordinary stuff of life shared with someone special. It's doing the dishes together, paying bills, watching television, laughing. Laughter is vital. Love is often not glamorous. You find it in the humdrum. Is this making sense?"

I nodded. Parents often assume their kids are stupid.

"It's a complex emotion," I said.

"Very true," said Mum. She started collecting plates. "And why have you become a 'student' of this particular subject?" I could hear the quotation marks.

"I think I'm in love," I said.

Mum's jaw dropped a little.

"But you're thirteen," she said.

"Is there an age limit involved?" I asked. "Am I barred, like trying to get in to watch a horror movie at the cinema?"

Dad folded the newspaper and rejoined the land of the living.

"Dad," I said. "The greatest, most wonderful love of your life?"

He didn't hesitate.

"Golf," he said.

1

BECAUSE I'M IN THE TOP ENGLISH CLASS AT SCHOOL,
I attended a writing workshop at a local literary festival a few
months back. It was run by a well-known writer for young
adults and children. I got a signed novel and I also learned
something about the techniques of writing a book (which
this is). She went on quite a bit about establishing a narrative
voice. I've been thinking long and hard about it.

*Hi! My name is Rob C. Fitzgerald (don't ask what the C
stands for—I'm not telling you on the grounds that it's hideous and embarrassing) and I'm thirteen years old.*

Then I remembered what the author had said about tone.
I looked at the word *"Hi!"* on the page. It struck me as way
too conversational and informal. I hit the backspace button.

*My name is Rob C. Fitzgerald (don't ask what the C stands
for—I'm not telling you on the grounds that it's hideous and
embarrassing) and I'm thirteen years old.*

I put my head in my hands. Think. Be critical. Are the brackets and the words in them necessary? If I'm not going to say what the C stands for (and trust me, I'm not), then why mention it? A tip the writer gave came back to me: *the delete key is your best friend.*

My name is Rob Fitzgerald and I'm thirteen years old.

Yuck. Ugly. Keep it simpler still.

I'm Rob Fitzgerald and I'm thirteen years old.

Two "I'm"s in the same sentence. That's a basic mistake.

I'm Rob and thirteen.

Perfect. If I'm actually *determined* to be boring.

Look, maybe it's best if we pretend this first chapter doesn't exist. If I don't get any better as a writer, you have permission to come to my house, tie me to a chair, and have at my toes with a blowtorch.

Which is way better than getting your money back if you're not entirely satisfied.

2

DANIEL SMITH WAS WAITING FOR ME AT THE ENTRANCE
to school.

Daniel Smith *always* waits for me at the entrance to
school. Sometimes he also waits for me when school is over.
It depends.

*Descriptive note: Daniel Smith. Age: fourteen (or thereabouts—
we don't exchange birthday cards). Stocky, but not like a good beef
stew. Solid and muscular, with red hair that sticks up at strange
angles. This makes his face resemble a drawing of a rising sun
completed by a three-year-old. Daniel is short, knows it, and
tries to compensate by being a bully, especially to me. He has
freckles and a way of standing, with his hands clenched at his
sides, arms forming brackets to his torso, that makes him look
like he's on the verge of pooping his pants. He has a habit of
sticking his chin out as if it was a weapon.*

"Hey, Fitzgerald," he growled, his loaded chin barely an

inch from mine, "gonna fight me, huh? Whaddya say? Cat got yer tongue? Gonna fight me, huh?"

Daniel is a fan of repetition. He is also a fan of the phrase "Cat got your tongue?" It is one of his favorite taunts, because I rarely talk at school unless I *really* have to. Most of the time, I keep quiet. Daniel finds me irritating, and my shyness makes things worse.

I tried to edge past him. If I could make it onto school grounds, then a teacher on yard duty would spot us. Unfortunately, Daniel was wise to this and blocked my path.

"C'mon, Fitzgerald," he said. "Be a man, all right? Man up." He laughed in my face, which was horrible since his breath comes straight from a baboon's bottom. He also loves demanding that I "be a man." Daniel obviously thinks this is hilarious, which is proof that he's a few toppings short of a decent pizza.

"Tellya what. You can have first punch. C'mon. Can't say fairer than that. Go on. First punch."

I tried to stand my ground, despite his breath. We'd had the same confrontation for months. Here is what I *wanted* to say: *I am never going to fight you, Daniel, because all of human history teaches us that fighting solves nothing.* But I kept my head down.

"Cat got yer tongue?" Daniel's voice dripped with contempt. "Unless you want me to beat yer head in here and now, then say something. Doesn't matter what. C'mon. Be a man. Just one word." He poked me on the shoulder. "Or can't you speak?"

"No," I mumbled.

"Hah, loser," he chortled. "You said you can't, but you used a word to say you can't. Ha—"

"Is there a problem here, guys?" It was Miss Pritchett, who has a nose for sniffing out potential fights, like a sixth sense. She'd appeared outside the school gates, which was impressive even for an expert battle bloodhound.

"No, Miss," said Daniel.

"No, Miss," I said.

"Fabulous," she said. "Then please come in, and mill around aimlessly until the bell rings. It's what students do."

We came in and milled around aimlessly until the bell rang. But Daniel kept looking at me. His hands were clenched, his arms bowed, and his eyes narrowed. He was a boy who looked in desperate need of the toilet.

3

GRANDAD WAS WAITING FOR ME AFTER SCHOOL, WHICH
threw not just a wrench into Daniel's plans, but a whole toolbox.

*Descriptive note: grandfather on father's side. Name:
Patrick "Pop" Fitzgerald. Age: . . . ancient. Once referred to
himself as "older than God's dog." When pressed, admits to
being as old as his tongue and slightly older than his teeth.
He is a collection of wrinkles in a nest of grayness. Was once
in the armed forces and served in a war overseas, but never
talks about it. Has a puckered scar on his right arm that
might be a souvenir of conflict, but never talks about it. Lives
by himself in a two-bedroom apartment for seniors in an
old-age home. Refers to it as the "place where a bunch of old
farts hang around, waiting to die." Or, occasionally, "God's
waiting room." Was married to my grandmother (duh) but
she must have died a long time ago because he never talks
about her. Neither does Mum or Dad. Grandad uses bad*

language a lot and doesn't like many people. He likes me.

"Hello, Pop," I said. He was leaning on his cane and sucking at his teeth, which he does almost constantly. Often this results in a high-pitched whistling sound like the ancient kettle he puts on the hot plate back at his apartment. It's eerie.

"Hello, young Rob," he said. "Would you like to accompany your old grandad to a fast-food restaurant for an after-school snack?"

"Yes, please," I said.

"Tough," he said. "Never been in one and not starting now. Blankety places use blankety offal." (You perhaps need to know that he doesn't actually say "blankety"—use your imagination.)

"Awful?"

"Offal. Guts, brains, buttholes. Dip 'em in batter, deep fry 'em, serve 'em up. Blankety criminal, it is."

"Deep-fried buttholes?"

"Exactly."

"So why did you offer to take me?"

"Because I'm blankety kind and generous to a fault, that's why."

"So where *should* we eat, then?"

"Nowhere. I'm not made of blankety money, you know."

It takes a while to get used to Grandad. It's been thirteen years for me, and I'm still working on it. In the end, we strolled back to his place and he made me a cup of tea with the whistling kettle. He bustled about in a cupboard, sucking his teeth, so I had the whistle in stereo.

"Pop," I said. "I'm in love."

That stopped him bustling. And whistling. He turned to face me.

"Who with?"

"A girl."

He slapped his palm against his forehead.

"Well, I didn't think you were in love with a *boy*, yer blankety bozo. What's her name?"

"Destry."

"I beg your pardon?"

"Destry. Destry Camberwick."

"That's not a name. That's an eighties rock band."

"She's perfect."

"Well, her name isn't."

I sighed, probably quite dramatically. Grandad echoed me.

"C'mon, young Rob," he said. "I'll break open the Arnotts. You can dip 'em in yer tea and tell me all the sordid blankety details."

4

THE FIRST TIME I SAW DESTRY CAMBERWICK, I WAS hunched over a tricky math problem.

Unfortunately, for me all math problems are tricky. Ask me what six times two is, and I have to take my shoes and socks off. My tongue was probably sticking out of the corner of my mouth. The door to the classroom opened but I paid no attention. Then the voice of the principal forced me to look up.

"Good morning, class," she bellowed.

"Good morning, Miss Cunningham," we all chanted in a disgusting singsong voice. I say "we," but I only got as far as the first syllable of the second word before my tongue stuck itself to the roof of my mouth, which turned as dry as a camel's armpit. You see, Miss Cunningham was not alone. She'd brought an angel with her.

Descriptive note: Destry Camberwick. Age: thirteen (or

thereabouts). Height: perfect. Skin: perfect. Eyes: two, both perfect. Nose: one, situated between the perfect eyes, perfect. Hair: shining, perfect, and down to her shoulders, which are perfect. Ears: hidden beneath perfect hair but almost certainly perfect and almost certainly two in number. Voice: . . . no idea yet, but probably flawless.

"Please welcome a new student to the school and to your class," bellowed Miss Cunningham. Our principal is incapable of speaking in anything less than a roar, which makes assembly somewhat frightening and has been known to cause a few small and especially nervous students to wet themselves. She alternates between a roar and a bellow. Today it was bellow's turn. "This is Destry Camberwick and she has moved here from Western Australia. I know you will all make her feel very welcome while she settles in . . ."

She bellowed other things but I didn't hear them because a heavenly choir had started to sing, somewhere in the back of my brain. It was only after Miss Cunningham left that I realized Destry would have to sit somewhere in our class, and there were only two options. Next to Damian Pilling, who has a problem with body odor, or next to me. It seemed a no-brainer from my perspective, but the thought of her taking the seat next to me made my insides go all squishy and gurgly. What would I do if she said "Hi"? I'd probably crack the desk with my jaw and then slide onto the floor when my bones turned to jelly. They'd have to take me home in a bucket.

Ms. Singh, our classroom teacher, made Destry sit next to Damian, so my bones didn't liquefy. She probably figured that Damian might smell, but at least he was capable of striking up a conversation. I wasn't disappointed. It gave me the chance to stare at Destry for the rest of the lesson, and I couldn't have done that if she'd sat next to me. Well, not without being totally creepy.

I loved the way her perfect nose crinkled when she got a whiff of Pilling's armpit.

5

"DOES SHE KNOW HOW YOU FEEL?" ASKED GRANDAD.

"Get real, Pop," I said. "You know I avoid talking. And even if I plucked up the courage, what am I going to do? Walk up to her and say, 'I love you, Destry'? She'd think I'm a complete loser."

"You're blankety gutless," said Pop.

"No I'm not," I said. Then I thought about it. "Yes, I am," I added. "And a complete loser."

"So what do you hope is going to happen?"

"Well, the ideal situation is that Destry comes up to me, at recess, for example, and says, 'Hi. You're Rob and possibly the most gorgeous person I have ever seen. I realize I'm not worthy of you, but I just had to tell you that I am head over heels in love with you. Spurn me if you must, but I had to let you know.' And I'd give this really cool smile, you know, like this is something that happens to me a lot, and then I'd just walk away, but throw her a look over my shoulder, maybe give her a wink, just to let her know she had a chance. . . ."

Grandad dunked a cookie into his tea and then pointed it at me. The end fell off and hit the coffee table with a dull splat.

"Gutless *and* an idiot."

"Harsh, but true," I said.

"If we could stay in the real world for just a moment, young Rob," said Grandad. "Does she even know you exist? Have you talked to her, for example?"

"Grandad, you *know* I'm painfully shy."

"So, you haven't talked to her?"

"No."

"Has she ever looked at you?"

"I walked into a basketball post yesterday because I was staring at her and didn't see it. Made a loud clang and I sat on the floor."

"She saw that?"

"I imagine. I can't be absolutely sure because I had blood running into my eyes."

Grandad dunked another cookie and sucked on it while he thought. For the first time, it occurred to me that we humans end our days the same way we start them. Sucking on mush because our teeth aren't up to it. Pop closed one eye and pointed the cookie at me. The end fell off with another dull splat.

"You're going to have to make a bigger impression," he said. "Frankly, *any* kind of impression would be a start. Sports."

"Sports?"

"Impress her with your sporting ability."

"I don't have any."

Grandad ignored me. "Is there a school event coming up? A sports day, something like that, where you could power home in the blankety hundred-meter, trailing clouds of glory?"

There was only one sporting event on the horizon. When I told Pop about it, he nodded.

"Perfect," he said. "And I know what position you are going to play. She can't fail to notice you, which is a start. Do a good job, and the scales will fall from her eyes. Even if you don't do a good job, but you're brave, it'll work. You will appear to her as a god, young Rob. A god."

"You're crazy, Pop," I said. "There's no way I'm playing in that game."

"You are."

"I'm not."

"I'm glad we agree," said Pop. "Now that we have a campaign plan, let's go to the community room and you can give me your best guess as to who among the inmates is going to die next. I've got a good idea, but I'd be interested in your view."

"Grandad!" I said. "That's horrible."

"You're right," he said. "It's totally horrible that this is what passes for entertainment in this place. It's so bloody boring. I blankety hope it's me who's kicking the bucket next."

"Grandad!" I said again. He tries to shock me, and I try not to smile.

But it's hard.

6

I TALKED OVER GRANDAD'S PLAN WITH MUM AND DAD
that evening.

I'd given it some thought as I walked home, and although I still believed it was nuts, it didn't seem *quite* as nuts as when he'd first mentioned it. See, I really hate being the center of attention. I freeze when I'm aware that everyone is looking at me, or expecting me to say something in a public forum. I get severe panic attacks. Oral presentations are a classic example. My mouth goes dry and my legs tremble and I simply *can't* say anything. Now I have a medical certificate and the school has to find alternative methods of assessment.

Grandad's plan would mean plenty of eyes on me, but there were, to my way of thinking, two pluses. One, I'd be busy. I wouldn't be looking at them looking at me, which is guaranteed to bring on a panic attack. Two, I'd be part of a team. There'd be twenty-one other people to look at.

I'd be diluted. Like Kool-Aid.

Nonetheless, the whole notion was basically dumb. I figured Mum and Dad would destroy Grandad's idea, shred it with the argument that I am shy and have no talent in sports. Grandad doesn't listen, and I needed allies. Luckily, I can talk about pretty much anything to my parents, which I know is unusual, if not outright weird for a thirteen-year-old. Most kids my age roll their eyes if parents are even mentioned in passing, but I'm not like that.

The thing is, they're accepting of who I am. Most people are, if I'm honest, though there are one or two exceptions, Daniel being an obvious example. Anyway, I trust my parents so I got straight down to it while Mum dished up the lasagna.

"Pop thinks it would be a good idea if I tried to impress Destry with my sporting ability," I said.

"What sporting ability?" said Mum, and "Who on earth is Destry?" said Dad at the same time.

"Rob is madly and passionately in love with a girl at school. Destry Camberwick," explained Mum.

"And she doesn't even know who I am," I added. "So, according to Pop, I need to get her attention by doing crazily brave sporting stuff."

"But, Rob," said Mum. "Sports? Really? Write her a love poem—you're terrific at English, but no one could really say you're a sporty person."

A love poem. Brilliant idea. I filed it away for future use. This was going well. Not only was Mum making ally noises but she'd also come up with a practical suggestion.

"But that's the point," I said. "I'm a bit nerdy, but if I could show how brave I am by playing a physical sport in the most dangerous position on the field, no one could fail to be impressed, could they?" This is called being the devil's advocate and involves arguing the opposite of what you believe, to firm up your case.

Mum placed a bowl of salad in the middle of the table.

"I hate to rain on your parade," she said, "but people normally get picked for a sporting team on merit. You know, actually being good at sports, rather than being hopeless. A small point, but an important one, I feel. Isn't that right, Alan?"

"Destry Camberwick?" said Dad. "Isn't that an eighties rock band?"

I ignored him.

"You don't know for *certain* I'm hopeless at sports, Mum," I said. I wanted her to argue, but I was becoming a little tired of the confident assertion that I'm rubbish at anything physical. Mums are meant to be supportive under all circumstances.

"I've been to countless sports days at your schools, Rob," said Mum. "You used to get out of the egg-and-spoon race because you felt it was dangerous."

This was an outrageous lie.

She continued. "You said that if you fell, you would probably poke your eye out with the spoon and possibly insert an egg up a nostril."

Ah, yes. I remembered. So not an outrageous lie, then.

Actually, it still seemed to me a fair assessment of what is obviously a risky sport.

Nonetheless, I couldn't help but wonder if this was how everyone viewed me. Not just as a total loser, but a coward as well? Grandad had called me gutless, and I'd agreed, but I thought he'd been joking. Kind of.

"But you're older now," Mum continued. "You *might* cope with the egg-and-spoon race. Is that what you're thinking of entering?"

I decided to ignore her sarcasm. Assuming it *was* sarcasm.

"Actually, it's the annual soccer game between our school and St. Martin's," I said. I aimed for a cool tone. "They're really good—we haven't beaten them . . . well, ever, I think. And we are total rubbish. Last year they won fourteen–nil, and they weren't even trying in the second half. Our team couldn't find their goal with a GPS."

"I think I spot the flaw in your plan, Rob," said Mum, placing a slice of lasagna on her plate. "You want to impress a girl by being a hopeless part of a hopeless team? The pity factor will only get you so far, I'm afraid. Plus, even if your school is unbelievably bad at soccer, I'd still find it impossible to imagine they couldn't find someone better than you. No offense."

23

"Plenty taken," I replied. This was turning into a nightmare.

"Wasn't Destry the name of a famous gunslinger in the Wild West?" said Dad.

"No one wants to be the goalie," I continued. "James Walter *is*, and he told me he hates it. But he can't get out of it, since no one is prepared to replace him and the coach won't let him drop out. So if I volunteer, James will be thrilled and I'll be on the team."

"The goalie is the one who tries to stop the ball from going into the net?" said Mum.

"Correct."

"Then won't you seem an even bigger loser if you're the one picking it out all the time? And who's to say Destry will even see the game? She's probably not interested in sports."

An even bigger loser? I took a deep breath. "She won't have a choice," I said. "The whole school is forced to watch. And, okay, even if we lose twenty–nil, I'm bound to make some saves, aren't I? And she'll have to notice me. All the action will be taking place around me."

"What do you think, Alan?" said Mum.

"Or was *Destry PI* an American show from the seventies?"

"Dad," I said. "You've been very helpful. Thanks." At least he wasn't insulting me.

"Don't mention it," he said around a mouthful of lasagna. "It's what dads are for."

"And, anyway," I said. "I don't need your approval, Mum.

I'm going to do it. I am." This was obviously a time to prove myself to Mum and Grandad. I wasn't going to be a wimp all my life. It was time to break the shackles of everyone's preconceptions and show I was made of tough material, that I was not afraid of spoons, eggs, or even soccer balls.

I think I saw a small smile play across Mum's lips as she lifted a glass of water to her mouth, but I might have been wrong.

7

ANDREW HARRIS IS MY BEST FRIEND IN THE WHOLE world, so I texted him later when I was in bed.

Descriptive note: Andrew. Age: fourteen. Tall. Long dark hair in a center part. Oh, forget it. I'm getting tired of these descriptive notes. It's just Andrew, okay? Doesn't matter what he looks like. Well, not for our purposes.

Andrew, being my best friend in the whole world, obviously knows about my Destry obsession. In fact, he's already made suggestions, but they've been of the kind that Grandad first put forward.

"Just ask her out, mate."

"I can't."

"Why not?"

"What if she says no?"

"Then she says no. But what if she says yes?"

"She won't."

"Why not?"

"Because I'm not going to ask her."

"Why not?"

"What if she says no?"

It was a conversation that he admitted made him want to punch my lights out. I told him to get in line behind Daniel Smith. But Andrew (never call him Andy, unless you want to *really* irritate him) is something of an expert on what girls want. He's had three girlfriends to my certain knowledge, and he's only just turned fourteen. That's impressive. In fact, it's inconceivable. Anyway, he'd know if my plan was a good one.

Andrew. Thinking of being goalie in annual
soccer game to impress Destry with my
bravery and general macho qualities. What
do you think?

(I am always grammatical, even in texts. It's called having standards.)

Ru nuts

(Most people don't bother.)

Yes, but what do you think?

U cd get killed

27

Then she would be overcome with grief. A
great aphrodisiac.

Wot

Aphrodisiac. Like a love potion.

**Thort it was type of hair cut anyway no
matter cos ud b dead ya moron**

True. Plan depends upon my survival.
Plucky trooper. Brave against all the odds.
Heroic in the face of intense danger.

Mite work or u cd just ask her out

What if she says no? And don't spell
"might" like that, just to save one letter. Mr.
Lazy.

I went to sleep full of enthusiasm for the plan. But I also
decided to write the love poem before the game. From my
research on the position of goalkeeper (five minutes on the
Internet), I understood that severe brain damage was a real
possibility. The worst-case scenario would be that I turned
into Daniel Smith.

8

I LOVE MY SCHOOL. WHEN I FIRST ARRIVED, I HAD A problem with the school uniform but Mum and Dad sorted it out, and since then it's been great. Everyone is friendly. Sure, there are a couple of people like Daniel Smith, but you get them everywhere. And really, the only way to deal with the Daniels of this world is to ignore them.

No, Milltown High is awesome and exceptionally supportive.

I went to see Mr. Broadbent, the PE teacher, at recess. He was in the gym, supervising a bunch of kids playing basketball, but he sat down with me on the bleachers and let the game run itself.

I explained. He looked me up and down and whistled.

"Goalkeeper, Rob?" he said. "You know what they say?" I didn't, but figured he'd tell me. "You have to be mad to be a goalkeeper. You can get kicked in the head—you almost certainly *will* get kicked in the head. It's like a war zone in that penalty area. You have to be incredibly brave. Imagine there's a fifty-fifty ball coming toward you."

I tried, but as I had no idea what a fifty-fifty ball was (half ball, half something else?), I failed. So I just nodded.

"The center forward is thundering in, determined to get to the ball before you do. He's huge and mean, and *all* he cares about is scoring that goal. What are you going to do?"

I thought, *If it means that much to him, who am I to stand in his way?* But I figured this wasn't a wise response if I wanted to make the team.

"I make sure I get to the ball before he does," I said.

"Right. But you'll be diving headfirst into the ground, while he's coming in with studs up. Who's going to get injured?"

"Me."

"Right. Can you do that, Rob? Because if you can't, you're no use to the school soccer team."

"I can do it, Mr. Broadbent."

He sniffed. "Tell you what. The game is in a month. I want you on the oval three times a week after school for training. We'll see what you're made of."

Blood, I thought, *if what you said about goalkeepers is true. Blood but nothing in the way of brains.*

"I won't let you down," I said.

I let him down.

Well, for the first couple of training sessions. See, the

goals in soccer are really high and wide, and I'm not. I stood in the center, on the goal line (give me some credit for getting the terminology right), and looked to my right, left, and up. There were massive spaces, just waiting for a soccer ball to sail through. In fact, from my perspective, you'd have to be unlucky *not* to score. You'd have to hit it straight at me and hope there wasn't enough time for me to get out of the way. Mr. Broadbent placed a ball on the penalty spot and took a few paces back.

"Okay," he said. "We'll start with the simple stuff. I'll kick the ball a little to your right or left. No, wait. I'll tell you. It will be to your left."

"Don't go easy on me, sir," I said. "I can take it."

He ignored me. "You must get down, so as much of your body as possible is behind the ball. Understand? Like you're lying down and the ball is hitting your stomach. No way for it to go through you."

I nodded and jumped up and down on my toes a little. I saw a goalkeeper do that and thought it looked cool. (Small confession—for research purposes I watched an English Premier League game on the television. Professional goalkeepers are BIG, by the way. Blankety huge, as Grandad might say.)

Mr. Broadbent stepped up and side-footed the ball four or five feet to my left. He's obviously a man of his word. I can't pretend it went fast. In fact it went so slowly that I can remember all of my thought processes. I probably would have had time to write them down.

You can get that, Rob.

What did he say? Dive. No, he didn't say "dive." He said, "Get your body behind it."

But I could stick my foot out and kick it away. Come to that, I could walk over and sit on it.

He said lie down with your body behind the ball.

Yeah, but that would mean throwing myself onto the ground.

So?

So the ground looks really hard. I could hurt myself.

The ball is going slowly, but the way this debate is going, it will be past you before you know it.

So, get on the ground or stick your foot out?

Well, do something.

Oops! Too late. It's a goal.

I remember thinking that I would look like a complete idiot, watching the ball as it slid oh-so-slowly into the goal while I impersonated a statue. So even though it was way too late, I stuck my left foot out. This threw my balance off completely and I fell back hard on my butt, upright, legs splayed. The ball kissed the back of the net, but gently.

Mr. Broadbent put his head into his hands and laughed. But gently. Or he might have been crying. I was too far away to be certain.

9

ONE OF THE PROBLEMS WITH THE NAME DESTRY IS THAT
there aren't too many obvious rhymes.

"Vestry" springs to mind.

> *The first time I saw my love, my Destry*
> *Was in the vicar's room, the vestry.*

You see the problem? It's not even close to the truth.
"Camberwick" isn't much better.

> *I'm as happy with my Destry Camberwick*
> *As a dog is with its doggie stick.*

It's clear the sensible option would be to forget about
rhyme entirely. But I *like* rhyme.

There has to be a way.

10

"OKAY," SAID ANDREW. "YOU SEE THIS BALL?"

I did. We were in my back garden. It was at his feet and round, which was a dead giveaway. I nodded.

"All right," he continued. "Now listen carefully and use your imagination. I know you have a great imagination because you keep getting straight As in English and annoying everyone."

It was true.

"I'm going to kick this ball as hard as I can," said Andrew, "and do you know why?"

I didn't and confessed it.

"Because I hate Destry Camberwick and she is standing behind you—"

I turned because you never know, but this was an imagination thing.

"—and this ball is going to hit her straight in her stupid,

ugly face. There's only one person who can stop that from happening, Rob. Who is it?"

"Well, if we're being logical, it would be you, Andrew. Because if you choose not to do it . . ."

Andrew put his hands on his hips.

"Okay, me," I said. "I am the guardian, the keeper of her face."

"Only you."

"Only me."

"'I will not let her face suffer!' Say it."

"I will not let her face suffer!"

"Louder!"

"I WILL NOT LET HER FACE SUFFER."

Andrew took a couple of paces back and then kicked the ball. I should say that my best friend is a very good soccer player. (He's very good at all sports—one of the reasons, he claims, why he's so successful with girls. If he wasn't my best friend, I'd probably hate him.) The ball screamed toward me, to my right and at about head height.

Andrew was right. My imagination is such that English teachers discuss it enthusiastically in staff rooms, which probably only proves they should get out more. I could see the ball hurtling toward Destry's face—Destry's poor, sweet, perfect face—and there was no time to think. I had to act. I took off to my right like a springbok, or, if not a springbok, then some other animal known for being nifty at jumping. I spread my arms. I might even have shouted,

"I WILL NOT LET HER FACE SUFFER," but I can't swear to that.

Someone should have videoed the entire sequence. It would have looked splendid in slow motion.

The ball hit me in the face, ricocheted off our clothesline, and crashed through next door's bathroom window.

"Blankety hell," said Andrew. "Run."

We did, but my head was really hurting and one eye was already closing, so I only ran into the clothesline and knocked myself out. I don't know why I was running anyway. I lived there and Mum was watching us through the kitchen window, so it's not like I could establish an alibi that would stand up in court.

11

HERE'S A STORY FOR YOU. SIT CROSS-LEGGED AND PUT your thumb in your mouth if you want.

Once upon a time there was a policeman called John Gray and he lived in Scotland. John was an ordinary guy, but he had an extraordinary dog, called Bobby. Bobby was a Skye Terrier, a little bundle of fur. He loved John, and John loved him, but John died, as everyone must at some time or other. John's friends buried him in the yard of Greyfriars church. Soon after, the gardener found Bobby sitting on John's grave. This, everyone agreed, couldn't be allowed. Churchyards have to be kept neat and tidy, and dogs, especially Bobby, were neither. So the gardener chased him off and was quite nasty, because you have to be firm with animals and let them know who's the boss.

Bobby didn't know who the boss was.

He snuck back in and sat on his master's grave. He was

chased off again. He came back. Again. And again.

Eventually, the gardener's heart softened and he stopped chasing Bobby off. The man even started feeding him. Bobby stayed, keeping watch over John's grave for the next fourteen years until he died himself, as all animals must at some time or other.

This is a true story and you can look it up if you Google "Greyfriars Bobby."

It's an example (and there are many) of how love is wonderful and magnificent and mysterious.

12

EVERY SUNDAY I HAVE TO ACCOMPANY DAD ON A ROUND of golf.

This is nonnegotiable.

Dad argues it's an opportunity for a lovely stroll in pleasant surroundings, to breathe fresh air and chat. He sees it as a bonding exercise, but I suspect it's so he doesn't have to wheel or carry his golf clubs, which are staggeringly heavy. He also hopes I will undergo a miraculous conversion, fall in love with the game, and beg for membership at his club.

There's not a snowball's chance in hell of that happening.

Hitting a small ball great distances into an equally small hole while wearing bad clothing is not my idea of fun. If it's that important, you could just pick the ball up, walk the four hundred yards, and place it there manually. And you wouldn't have to wheel or carry staggeringly heavy golf clubs, which would be a huge bonus.

Dad stuck his tee into the ground on the first hole and balanced a ball on top of it. "Number one wood, please," he said.

I took the club out of the bag (it's impossible to do eighteen holes every Sunday and not understand which club is which). I even took off its little furry hat. Why do golf clubs need hats? It's not like they're liable to catch cold on wintry days. Perhaps it's a style thing, in which case it would be better to have tiny baseball caps that you could put on your five iron backward, to give it a gangsta attitude.

Dad took the club and "addressed" the ball. This has nothing to do with talking to it or even writing down where it lives, but involves him waggling his bottom, looking down at the ball, looking up toward where he's hoping to hit it, down at the ball again, up again, down again. Sometimes he stops waggling and takes a step back before resuming the position and going through the looking and waggling business again. It takes forever. Finally, he swings the club back and whacks the living daylights out of the ball. I didn't give him the chance this time.

"Dad?" I said. This was in the middle of his backswing. I know I shouldn't talk in the middle of his swing. Golfers get very annoyed when this happens. It's bad etiquette, like someone taking a poo on the floor in the middle of a crowded restaurant. I'm not sure if this has ever happened, though very little surprises me anymore.

The ball flew away, way off to our left. This is called a "hook," or it might be a "slice." I can't remember, but it's not good. Dad was angry.

"ROB! Never talk to me in the middle of my swing. You know better."

I did, but I was in a strange mood. He gave me the golf club and I put its hat back on, tucked it away into the bag, and started wheeling the trolley. Dad headed off in the general direction of where the ball had flown. I kept a pace or two behind him.

"Was it love at first sight when you met Mum?" I asked. "Did you hear music? Did your surroundings melt away as your vision focused on her across a crowded room, and did you bid your fluttering heart be still?"

Dad didn't pause and he didn't look back.

"I heard music," he said.

"You *did*?" I was thrilled.

"It was in a nightclub," he added. "You couldn't hear anything *other* than music. Heavy metal, I seem to recall."

"Oh." I gave this some thought. There's something spooky about realizing your parents were once young enough to go to nightclubs. A shiver ran up my spine. "What about your surroundings? Did they melt?"

"I hadn't had that much to drink."

"Dad. I'm serious."

It took a while, but I teased the details from him over the course of our eighteen holes, especially since it became obvious that unless he talked, I was going to ask him at crucial times, like when he was setting up an important putt.

This is his story.

13

DAD WASN'T ALWAYS BALD AND SHAPED LIKE A HOT-AIR
balloon (his description). When he was twenty, he was slim,
had a bizarre hairstyle, and could "bust amazing moves on
the dance floor." This was at a time when people called good
dancing "busting moves." Life is better now.

Anyway, Dad went out with a bunch of his mates to a
nightclub in Sydney where busting moves was the main aim,
along with drinking alcohol to excess and "chatting up birds."
(By the way, I asked for a translation of "chatting up birds,"
and it refers to impressing women with your conversational
skills. Never saying "chatting up birds" or "busting moves"
would be a good start, but I didn't mention this to Dad.)

To cut a long and disappointingly boring story short,
Dad met Mum on the dance floor. She was a bird and he
chatted her up. They busted moves together.

"So, no gazing across a crowded floor?" I asked.

"She bumped into me and I spilled my beer down her dress."

"Did your heart sing?"

"It sank. I couldn't afford another beer."

"Love at first sight?"

"Got her name wrong for a couple of weeks. Kept calling her Sandra." Mum's name is Catherine.

"When you proposed, did you get down on one knee?"

"I sent her a card saying, 'Fancy making it legal?'"

"Dad! Where's the romance in that?"

"It must've taken the day off."

At some stage Dad saw the expression on my face and realized that what he thought was jokey good fun was upsetting me. He sat me down on a bench close to the fourteenth hole and waved the players behind us through. This was a huge sacrifice and I knew it.

"Mate," he said. "I'm joking with you. Don't cry."

It was true. I'd started sobbing and hadn't even realized it. I'm such a crybaby. It's embarrassing.

"So that's not how you met Mum?"

"That's *exactly* how I met your mum," he said. He put his arm around my shoulders. "And I'm sorry you find it so . . . disappointing. But I'm telling you the truth. There were no orchestras playing, no rays of light beaming on us, no hearts popping, no . . . romance. I didn't love her at first sight. She didn't love me at first sight either. In fact, I think she thought I was something of an idiot."

"But . . ."

"But here's the thing. Once I met your mum, I never looked at another woman again. Never felt the need, never got the urge. If she was to leave me or, heaven forbid, die, it would be as if my life lost all meaning, as if . . . I was living in a dark hole. She's the first person I think about when I wake up and the last person I think about when I go to sleep."

"Dad," I said. "That's so romantic."

"I don't know about romantic, but it's true," he said. "Now, can I finish this bloody round of golf, please? I am not waving any other players through."

14

"I'VE BEEN THINKING," SAID ANDREW.

I resisted the urge to make the obvious joke. But not for long.

"Does it hurt?" I said.

"What do you actually *know* about Destry Camberwick?" We sat on a bench in the school cafeteria. Through a mass of bodies I caught the occasional glimpse of Destry's form as she sat, with a couple of friends, on a distant bench of her own. It hadn't taken her long to settle in to Milltown High. To become popular, too, judging by the company she was keeping. That was a good sign in a way, because obviously she wasn't boring. But also a bad sign. There would doubtless be competition for her affections, and I could really do without any competition at all.

"I know she's gorgeous," I replied.

"Yeah. You've said. Like a couple of million times."

Andrew tucked into his burger. I toyed with my fries. Those occasional glimpses of Destry had made me lose my appetite. "But you're not a shallow person, Rob," he added.

"I might be."

"You can't fall in love with someone just because of their looks."

"I did."

"I'm ignoring you," he said, which was a sensible tactic under the circumstances. "You know as well as I do that a person is much more than their physical appearance. Take you, for example. No one could say you're fantastically good-looking . . ."

"Couldn't they?"

". . . yet when I got to know you, I realized that beneath your ugly face . . ."

"Hey!"

". . . lurks a fine and splendid person."

"My face wasn't ugly until you starting hitting it with high-speed soccer balls."

Andrew started on my fries. He picked one up and pointed it at me, but the effect was ruined because it was soggy and just drooped in a sad fashion.

"Destry could be an airhead. She could be racist or homophobic. You need to find out if the two of you are compatible."

I nodded. "There's no art to find the mind's construction in the face," I said.

Andrew threw the fry at me.

"Are you quoting Shakespeare at me again?"

"Guilty," I said. "*Macbeth*."

"Stop it," he said. "Just when I think you can't be any more annoying, you do stuff like that."

"I thought you said I was a fine and splendid person?"

"I was lying."

I thought for a few moments. Andrew was right. I knew that. What's more, everything that Mum and Dad had said about the nature of love confirmed it. It wasn't about physical appearance. It was about . . . what had Mum said? *Doing the dishes together . . . the ordinary stuff of life.*

"What you're saying, Andrew," I said, "is that I need to find out if I can do the dishes with Destry Camberwick."

"Shut up, Rob. Okay?"

"Okay."

"So," Andrew continued. "I'm going to be your wing-man, your research man, the insider, the mole burrowing beneath the surface of the Camberwick. I'll find out what makes her tick, what music she likes, what TV shows she watches, what her hobbies are. Information is power, my friend, and you need information."

This was obviously the best idea in the world. Find out her taste in music? I could download the songs she liked and have them blasting from my earphones as I casually strolled past her. Talk in a loud voice about how I *loved* . . . whatever TV show she happened to be into. It was perfect. But then another thought struck me.

"That will mean you'll spend a lot of time talking to her."

"Yeah. And her friends. You know I get along well with girls."

I threw the soggy (and by now almost disintegrated) fry back at him. "Yeah," I said. "I do. They love you. Destry will love you. And you'll love Destry." I could see it all unfolding in my horrified imagination. Destry and Andrew eloping at the end of term. Andrew sending me a letter from somewhere far away, like Paris, telling me how sorry he was but that he and Destry were setting up house, even though he was fourteen and she was thirteen, and how they would name their first kid after me . . .

"Are you crazy?" said Andrew. He looked for another fry to throw, but we'd run out.

"It's possible."

"You're my best friend," he said. "I would never do that to you. Anyway, she's not my type."

"All girls are your type," I pointed out.

"Not true. I am not that shallow."

I thought about it. If Destry Camberwick fell in love with Andrew, there was almost certainly nothing I could do about it. And if she did, it was probably a good thing if I found out about it sooner rather than later. But if she didn't and he didn't, the advantages could be huge. Maybe I should trust my best friend.

"Okay," I said. "When are you going to start?"

"No time like the present," he said, and headed off to the far reaches of the cafeteria. I watched until my vision was blocked by a stocky form.

"Wanna fight me, Fitzgerald?" said Daniel. "Huh? Cat got yer tongue? Wanna fight? C'mon. Be a man . . ."

"Is there a problem here?" said Miss Pritchett, materializing out of thin air.

15

"MY BLANKETY MONEY'S ON AGNES," SAID GRANDAD.

"I am *not* betting with you on who's going to die next, Pop," I replied. "That's in appallingly bad taste."

"That's exactly why I love the game. I'm not sure what your blankety problem is, Rob."

We sat in a couple of comfortable armchairs in the old folks' common room. According to Grandad, this was the social hub of the entire institution. They played bingo, there was a piano (which one of the residents played most evenings—Pop was of the opinion that if someone broke his fingers, they'd be doing the community a great service), but they also had guest artists turn up from time to time. A month ago, they'd had a juggler from a traveling circus. Next week they were getting art lessons. The residents might be, in Pop's poetic phrase, "a bunch of old farts waiting to die," but they were generally having fun while they waited.

"I need to borrow a dog, Pop," I said.

"Of course you do," said Grandad. "Remind me why again."

"Because Destry Camberwick has a dog she takes to the park the same time every night." Andrew had come up with the goods that very first day. Destry was a dog lover. It was terrific intelligence and I was determined to use it to my advantage. "It's the perfect opportunity for me to 'accidentally' stumble across her while walking my own dog," I added.

"You haven't got a dog."

"Which is why I need to borrow one, Pop. Hello?"

"Ah, yes."

"Having stumbled across Destry Camberwick, it will then be a simple matter to strike up a conversation."

Destry: Wow. I love your dog. What's his name?

Me: Chopper. And what's your Pekinese/boxer/Labrador/ heeler called?

Destry: Rob.

Me: What a coincidence! That's my name!

Destry: That's amazing. It's obvious we were destined to meet, fall in love, have five children, and be happy and fulfilled together!

Me: So what are we waiting for?

Grandad sucked at his teeth, which set off the whistling. It sounded like "Waltzing Matilda," but that was probably just my imagination.

"Conversation is not your strong suit, young Rob," Grandad pointed out.

"I know. But I'm going to have to get over it." It was true. I was facing death by soccer ball, so I believed it was possible to change.

"A lot of the old farts here have dogs," said Grandad. "When you get to my age, it suddenly seems like a good idea, apparently. No idea why."

"Maybe they love the dog and the dog loves them."

"Unlikely. This is God's waiting room and these are old farts, remember."

"You can love an old fart. You're one and I love you."

"This conversation is getting blankety revolting, young Rob. I told you it wasn't your strong suit, so stop it."

We sat in silence for a couple of minutes. I said hello to a few of the residents. I'd been here so often, I was getting to know everyone. I even found myself eyeing up Agnes to see if Pop's prediction was a long shot or not. She *did* look pale . . .

"Jim's got a dog," said Pop. "And he's a bit unsteady on his legs, so he'd probably be happy if you could take it for a walk."

"Fabulous," I said. "Can you ask him for me?"

"You blankety ask him. Consider it conversational practice, because God knows you need it."

Borrowing Jim's dog was not a problem. Pop talked to him and so did I. To be honest, it was something of a small miracle he remembered even having a hound. Or his own name. I arranged to come around the following day at four thirty to pick the pooch up. Destry's routine was to hit the local park between five and five thirty, and I was going to be there, all casual, dog-lover-like, and generally irresistible.

I had a good feeling about this. Between that and the brilliant goalkeeping performance to come, I was going to be hot property.

I almost started fancying myself.

16

"WHAT'S HAPPENED IN THE LAST FEW DAYS?" MR. Broadbent was astonished. I knew this because he added, "I'm astonished."

"I've been practicing," I said. I stood on the goal line and waved my goalkeeping gloves above my head. They were huge and I was probably a dead ringer for Mickey Mouse. With the exception of the ears. Maybe not with the exception of the ears. Andrew's words about my physical appearance had cut deep.

"You've been . . . exceptional today, Rob," Mr. Broadbent said. "Absolutely phenomenal."

I had to agree.

Andrew clearly has a future as a motivational speaker when he grows up. His words about protecting Destry's face were now inscribed onto my brain. When the ball hurtled toward me, all I could see was her face in its trajectory, her beautiful nose squished. And I could not let it happen. I threw myself from one side to the other. I tipped the ball over the bar, pushed it around the post. On the few occasions when Mr. Broadbent allowed other players to try to score against me, I charged straight at them and blocked the ball any way I could. My arms, my legs, my feet. My face. Nothing mattered. I would die to stop that ball from getting past me.

I spent an hour in practice. I did not allow one goal to be scored. Suck on *that*, Mum.

"You're on the team," said Mr. Broadbent when he finally blew the whistle for the end of training. "Blankety hell. We could even win this year. Well, get a draw. In all honesty, our forwards couldn't find the opposition's goal with a GPS."

17

I ARRIVED AT THE PARK AT EXACTLY FIVE TO FIVE. IT'S
only a two-minute walk from Grandad's place to the park,
but there were problems when I arrived to pick up Jim's dog.
Jim had forgotten I was coming, for one thing, and had to be
tracked down in the far reaches of the grounds, where the staff
found him talking to a random duck. Then we had to find the
dog. This was not as easy as might be expected, but eventually
we discovered it in another resident's room—Agnes, actually,
who told us she'd taken over the upkeep of the pup when it
became obvious that Jim was not up to the job.

The dog was called Trixie, and it was a fluffy bundle
of rubbish. These are not my words, I hasten to add, but
Agnes's.

"I hate FBRs," she said. "Little, nasty, yapping things, like
pipe cleaners on steroids." I didn't say anything because I didn't
know what a pipe cleaner looked like. I was a bit vague on the

subject of steroids as well. It didn't matter, because Agnes was on a roll. "Think they're tough, and yet an average cat could eat one. An overestimated sense of their own importance. A bit like my first husband. And my second. . . ." She waved a hand as if to dismiss husbands in general. "Yet she *is* a dog. Only just, true, but a dog nonetheless. And therefore better than ninety-nine percent of humanity." She poked me in the chest with a bony finger, which was a little harsh since I hadn't even tried to argue with her. "A dog loves you and it has no agenda," she said. "Treat it badly, ignore it, even abuse it, God help us, and a dog will still think you are the greatest thing ever. People are disgusting. Dogs are beautiful."

I glanced at Grandad.

"Okay," he said. "Maybe I was wrong. Maybe it'll be Jim next."

"What?" said Agnes.

"Nothing," said Pop and I together.

"Well, come on," she said. "Are you simple, or what? Trixie might be a fluffy bundle of rubbish but she loves her walks." She handed me a short leash and a couple of poo bags. "Craps like a good one too," she added.

Trixie wasn't the easiest dog in the world to control. Agnes was right. This pooch was tiny, but it seemed to have no idea that, in potential conflict situations, it was at a severe disadvantage. It barked at cars. It yapped at motorcycles. If it had been anatomically capable, it would probably have given a tattooed biker the finger and said, *C'mon, pal. Think you can take me? Bring it on.*

I tried to steer it around the pathways of the park, but other dog owners were doing the same thing and Trixie appeared to take the presence of another dog as a personal insult. It was Trixie's park. It was her patch. Like a drug dealer, she resented competition and was happy to show it. I spent most of my time apologizing.

Then I saw Destry Camberwick. She turned a corner, and an orchestra played, my peripheral vision disappeared, and I saw her as if through a tunnel, radiant, splendid, and impossibly perfect. Then I saw her dog and the orchestra gave up.

Holy moly. This thing was enormous. I'm not an expert on dog breeds, but this was probably *Houndus blankety-maximus.* I've seen smaller wrestlers on the TV. It loped along, blotting out the sun and causing distinct tremors each time a paw hit the sidewalk. Its muscles had muscles. I glanced down at Trixie.

She had a gleam in her eye, as if, finally, a challenge worthy of her had been presented. I had a bad feeling about this.

Destry and I were on a collision course, which suited me fine. It didn't suit Trixie. She twisted on her leash and went into a frenzy of yelping. Imagine a tiny, tiny person possessed by the devil, and you will get some idea of her anger. She strained at the leash. *Let me at him*, her body language shouted. *Think you're tough, mate? I'll kick your butt.*

Destry's dog sat down and cocked its head. I was

becoming an expert dog translator. *What's this funny fluffy bundle of rubbish? How amusing. Is it dinner or merely an appetizer?*

I smiled at Destry, who smiled back. Maybe this could work to my advantage. I opened my mouth to speak and suddenly went all clammy and light-headed. This was absurd. I *can* talk, after all. It's just a matter of exerting control.

"I'm sorry," I said finally, and I don't think my voice trembled at all. "She doesn't know her own strength."

It was obvious that Destry had no idea who I was. Even walking into a basketball post at school and bleeding all over the court hadn't attracted her attention. I almost gave up then. But I didn't. Her smile faded and she went to walk past me. I knew I had to find something to keep her there.

If I'm honest, I'm not at my best under pressure.

"M-my dog could kill your dog," I stammered at her back (which, incidentally, was perfect).

That stopped her.

"I'm sorry?" she said, turning to face me. The first words I'd ever heard her speak. It was music to my ears. Much better than music. It was angels singing.

"I think my dog can kill your dog," I repeated.

She looked at me. Her dog looked at me. Trixie finally stopped yelping and looked at me. Something was required but I had no idea what it might be. So I tried a wider smile.

"An explanation would be good," said Destry.

"Absolutely," I said, nodding like a maniac. She had a

point, and I only wished someone could supply it.

"Well?" she said.

"Fine, thanks. And you?"

"No. The explanation."

"Pardon me?" Even I found my pathetic attempt to buy time embarrassing.

"How could your dog kill my dog?" she said.

"Ah, that." I looked at her dog and I looked at mine. A few seconds passed.

"Suffocation," I said. "If Trixie got stuck in its throat."

I was dragging myself (and Trixie) back to Grandad's place. My eyes were fixed firmly on the sidewalk, my gaze as low as my spirits, when a shadow fell across the path and stayed there. I looked up.

"Wanna fight me, Fitzgerald? Huh? Wanna fight? Come on, be a man. Tellya what, I'll give you first punch. Whaddya say? Cat got yer tongue?"

I opened my mouth, but nothing came out.

"Fancy seeing you guys here," came a familiar voice. "Is everything fine? Are we hunky-dory?"

"Yes, Miss Pritchett," said Daniel Smith.

"Yes, Miss Pritchett," I said, even though I had only a vague understanding of the meaning of "hunky-dory." I'd be prepared to bet that Daniel thought it was a type of fish.

"Good," she said. "Run along, then."

We ran along. In opposite directions, which suited me fine.

18

"ANDREW?" I SAID.

He grunted, which is sometimes all you can get from Andrew early in the morning.

"Do you think Miss Pritchett has superpowers?"

"What are you on about?"

I shrugged. "I dunno. Maybe supersensitive hearing? Or a psychic connection. An ability to transport herself across time and space, when she senses someone is in trouble and needs immediate assistance. X-ray vision . . ."

"I worry about you sometimes, mate," said Andrew. "I really do. Sometimes I wake up in a cold sweat worrying about you."

"Seriously?"

"No."

"But—"

"Shut up, Rob."

"Okay."

I needed to think anyway. It was time to reevaluate my strategies. I'd had three. Firstly, I was going to impress the hell out of Destry with my sporting ability. That was still a possibility. The soccer game was tomorrow and I'd been improving day by day. The poem was backup, but that was proving tricky. I could write essays. I could write short stories. I could even write poems about life, the universe, and the futility of existence. But I couldn't write a poem about how Destry Camberwick made me feel.

Then there was the dog lover business, which hadn't started well. True, she had spoken to me. Eighteen brilliant words that would live forever in my memory. *An explanation would be good.* Was there a secret message in that statement? Was she trying to tell me something? It was possible.

"Andrew?" I said. He'd told me to shut up, but this was important. He knows about girls and what makes them tick. If anyone could answer this, it would be Andrew.

He grunted.

"When a girl says 'an explanation would be good' when you tell her your dog could kill hers, is she trying to say anything? You know, a secret meaning?"

"Rob. Shut up."

"Okay." I took that as a no and went back to my strategies.

I'd probably have to give up on walking Trixie. True, it would give me the perfect excuse to keep bumping into Destry, but the difference between our canines was too extreme. They say a dog is a reflection of its owner. Would dragging around a fluffy bundle of rubbish that barked hysterically make Destry view me as someone lightweight, someone who had no idea how pathetic he looked? Maybe that wasn't too far from the truth. I was not in Destry's league, just as Trixie wasn't in . . . whatever the hell league Destry's dog was in. The "massive mastiff that could be mistaken for an elephant" league. Then again, if Destry was like her dog, maybe it wasn't a great idea to get involved. She could kill me. But what a way to go. . . .

"I think you need something else," said Andrew. I waited. He'd told me to shut up and I respected that. He pointed at me. "The soccer is good. I've been watching your practices. I can't believe how well you've played! Do what you've been doing in the game tomorrow, and she can't help being impressed."

"Really?"

"Guaranteed. So, you could have the sporty business worked out." He held up a hand and ticked off the points. "Sports, one." He straightened another finger. "The poetry. Great idea. You are the English genius of Milltown High and no girl can resist a romantic poem."

I could have quoted the bits about the vestry and the doggie stick but felt it was better to keep quiet.

"The dog walking shows you're kindred souls as far as animal loving is concerned." He put up a third finger. "But your dog's a bit lame, from what you've said. Could you borrow another one that's more like hers?" It was spooky how

Andrew's analysis was so close to mine. Then again, as I might have mentioned, we *are* best friends. But I'd considered this idea and rejected it.

"Nah," I said. "Firstly, it's not a good look if you keep changing dogs like underwear. I mean, an animal lover would definitely think that's suspect. Plus, I don't think there *are* any other dogs like the one Destry has. It's a mutant, Andrew. I've seen trucks that are smaller. I—"

"Okay. Maybe it's enough that you've shown her you're a pet person. But . . ." He flipped up a fourth finger. "What about the inner person, Rob?"

"You've lost me."

"Sporty, book lover, animal lover, but what about your *beliefs*? Your values? Your spirituality?"

"What about them?"

"I think you need a passion. Maybe a political stance. Something that shows that beneath the brilliant sportsperson, the talented poet, and the dog fanatic there lurks a caring soul, someone who has a drive to make the world a better place."

"I *do* want the world to be a better place, Andrew," I said.

"Then show us, show her, how you plan to do it."

He's a smart one, Andrew. And little did I know his words would change my life completely.

Did I mention we are best friends?

I was fast asleep when my phone pinged. Text message.

I fumbled for the light switch. Eleven forty-two. Who the

hell was texting me at this time of night? The number was displayed in the notification box, indicating this was not from anyone in my contact list. I opened the message.

Do not fear fear. Its only purpose is to let you know that something is worth doing.

May fortune smile on you in the game tomorrow, Rob.

I texted back.

Who is this?

Even though I stayed awake for another half hour, I didn't get a reply.

19

THE DAY OF THE GAME. MILLTOWN HIGH VERSUS ST.
Martin's. This year it was at our school, not that home
advantage had ever *been* an advantage in the long history of
our annual matches. Basically, the game is rigged.

See, Milltown is an ordinary public school. It's great. Don't
get me wrong. Its students have a huge range of academic
abilities and an equally huge range of ethnic backgrounds.
This *makes* it great. All of human life is here. St. Martin's,
on the other hand, is a private school. It charges massive
fees and in return promises excellence, though its gradua-
tion rates aren't quite as good as ours. The excellence comes
in facilities. An amazing library, partly paid for by someone
in the government who used to go there. An Olympic-sized
swimming pool that was opened by Ian Thorpe himself. A
state-of-the-art lecture and performing arts theater that can
hold a thousand people.

Our school relies on portables, and some of those are riddled with asbestos.

No one really knows how the St. Martin's versus Milltown soccer game started in the first place, or why it's become an annual tradition. Maybe it was as simple as the people with money wanting assurance they were superior to those without. If true, they'd got plenty. Milltown had never beaten St. Martin's. *Never.* In the last five years the scores had been 15–0, 17–0, 21–0, 24–0, and 14–0. At least we improved last year. And why this dreadful drubbing? Because St. Martin's has a custom-built soccer ground and training gym, a specialist manager who'd once been an assistant coach for the national under-seventeens, and a sports psychologist. Milltown has losers like me and a small shack on the oval that passes for a changing room, and smells of pee.

I thought about injustice as we watched the St. Martin's team step down from their customized bus. The Socceroos would have been jealous of the transport. You see, I also know that St. Martin's receives more government funding per student than our school does, and we have plenty of kids with special needs. Depending on who you talk to, that includes me. And St. Martin's charges an additional twenty-five thousand dollars a year in fees. We ask for fifty bucks from parents to buy books for the library, though few cough up.

No wonder they kick our sorry butts.

The whole system is rigged.

20

"GRANDAD," I SAID. "I NEED SOMETHING TO BELIEVE IN."

"Me too," Pop replied. "I believe I'll have another beer." He grabbed one from his fridge, unscrewed the cap, and took a long swig.

"I'm serious."

"Me too. I never joke about beer."

I sat on Grandad's couch and gazed out the window. It was a gorgeous afternoon and the grounds at the old-age home are splendid, even beautiful. Paths weave between garden beds, and there is a slightly dysfunctional fountain in the central lake. Even at this distance I could make out Jim talking to a duck. It was peaceful. Not the duck, which seemed slightly agitated. Or maybe puzzled.

"Is there one single thing," I asked, more to myself than anyone else, "that could be easily done to make the world a place less full of suffering and inequality?"

"Of course there blankety is," said Grandad. "Simplest thing in the world."

I waited, but he appeared to be done. He sat in the chair opposite me, stared at the wall, and sucked on his teeth. I had to ask, if only to stop the whistling.

"And that is?"

"What?"

"What is it?"

"What's what?"

"I don't know why I talk to you sometimes, Pop," I said, not even trying to keep the exasperation out of my voice. I would almost have welcomed the return of the whistling.

"Neither do I."

I took a deep breath.

"What is the simplest thing to make the world less full of suffering and inequality?"

"Vegetables," said Grandad.

"Vegetables?" I said. I knew I shouldn't, because it only encourages him.

"And I'm not talking about the inmates here in the Old Farts' Palace. I'm talking vegetarianism. I'm talking about how meat eaters like you are destroying the planet."

He suddenly leaned forward and pointed his beer bottle at me.

"Do you know what I think is the biggest blankety lie spread around by people who should know better?" I opened my mouth to answer, but that apparently wasn't necessary. "It's that young people are better informed, have greater access to news and information than any generation in history. Frankly, Rob, you're a bunch of blankety idiots who couldn't find your own buttholes with a flashlight and a road map."

"Thanks for the vote of confidence, Pop."

"Do you *ever* watch the news? On television or probably on those blankety phones you seem to have superglued to your fingers?"

"Of course I do," I said. Indignation was definitely present in my tone. "Well, no, come to think about it. Not much."

"Well, get on your Raspberry phone or your iPatch and Goggle it. 'What would happen if the whole world became vegetarian?' Go on, Goggle it. You'll be amazed."

I did.

I was.

21

THE WHOLE SCHOOL TURNED UP FOR THE GAME BECAUSE they didn't have a choice.

Most of St. Martin's came along as well, in about fifty chartered buses. Their fans clutched little pennants with the St. Martin's flag and motto emblazoned on them. Their motto is, of course, in Latin, and translates as "We have poo-loads of money and are much better than you nasty working-class kids." Milltown High can't afford a motto, even one in English, but if we could, it would probably be "Wassup?"

Their students took up all the seating on one side of the pitch. We couldn't afford seating all the way around so, being good hosts, we let them have what was available. This meant spectators had to stand in the mud on the touchline opposite the St. Martin's fans, tiniest students at the front and seniors toward the back. St. Martin's waved their little pennants and looked cheery, probably because they were going to make an effort this year and score forty goals. Our supporters had a haunted look. If you had offered them a forty–nil scoreline before we started, they would've taken it, if only so we could all go home.

I went onto the pitch early because the rest of my teammates were getting changed. I'd been wearing my kit under my school uniform all day, which had been bloody hot. I tried to spot Destry Camberwick but couldn't. I saw Andrew, though. He gave me a huge thumbs-up. I would have preferred full-body armor or, failing that, a large hole to swallow me up. Now that the match was only minutes away, I was fighting to keep a panic attack at bay. I didn't so much have butterflies in my stomach as wedge-tailed eagles.

I closed my eyes and concentrated on my breathing.

The players from both sides trooped out to join me, and we lined up on the halfway line to sing the Australian anthem. Well, St. Martin's did. None of my team knew the words, apart from "let us rejoice" and "girt by sea," which only gets you so far and therefore involves a lot of mumbling. Then we shook hands.

That's the thing about St. Martin's. Maybe it's the thing about all private schools. They give the impression of being civilized and decent and friendly, but up close the truth is revealed. These kids (and some of them looked as if they played prop forward for the Kiwi national rugby team in their spare time or had jobs as nightclub bouncers) tried to crush our hands when they shook them. They gazed deep into our eyes as if what they really wanted was to stick their hands down our throats and turn us inside out. Maybe that's where the sports psychologist came in. After we'd shaken their hands, I could tell our entire team felt terrified and defeated. On the sidelines, the St. Martin's students chanted the school song. Our side looked as if they'd sooner be in math class working on differential equations.

We won the toss (the only thing we *could* win—we should have called it a day there and then) and elected to kick off. I think we did this so we could at least say we had the ball in their half once. I trotted back to my goal and jumped up and down on my toes. I still couldn't see Destry, but I did spot Grandad. He'd asked the principal if he could watch the match and had been politely refused (as politely as a roar or bellow would allow). It was open only to students and staff, he'd been informed. Couldn't let all parents and relatives come as there simply wasn't room. So sorry. Hope you understand. Grandad certainly understood. It's just that he didn't care. As he expressed it to me later, *What are they gonna do? Taser me and drag me off school grounds, an eighty-year-old war veteran with a bad hip? That'll look blankety great on the evening news.* So he was there and, as far as I could tell, had avoided being Tasered. I was really pleased to see him, which goes to show how desperate I was.

The referee blew his whistle. Our center forward kicked it straight to the opposition and St. Martin's poured forward in attack.

I was very busy for the next ninety minutes. I mean *busy*.

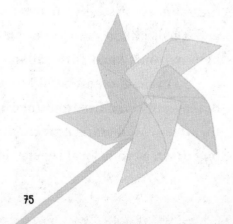

22

SO, WHAT WOULD HAPPEN TO THE WORLD IF EVERYONE
became vegetarian?

The production of livestock for human consumption generates a third of all greenhouse emissions worldwide. A third!

An average American family of four emits more greenhouse gases because of the meat they eat than from driving two cars. People talk about cutting back on car usage (and so they should), but no one talks about cutting down the number of steaks on the grill. There are about one and a half billion cows on earth, and each cow produces between thirty and fifty gallons of methane a day. That is . . . I'm no good at math, I've already told you . . . a *lot* of methane. It comes from their manure, their burps, and their farts. Methane is a greenhouse gas. So, that steak you buy down at your local supermarket is making the planet warmer because of its history of poos, burps, and farts.

Livestock takes up a huge amount of space that could be used for other things. There are about twelve billion acres of agricultural land available in the world. Nearly seventy percent of that is used for rearing livestock that we then eat. One third of the crops we *do* produce worldwide goes straight down the throats of those animals, to fatten them up. If that land was used for other crops, it could feed the hungry of the world. Nearly a billion people struggle with hunger every day. Each year more than two and a half million children die from hunger-related causes. They die, in large part, because we in first world countries want to eat meat.

I haven't even mentioned animal cruelty yet. But I will. You can trust me on that.

I learned all of this in ten minutes.

I Goggled it on my iPatch.

23

LISTEN. THE MEMBERS OF OUR SOCCER TEAM ARE ALL fine, upstanding kids with a wide range of talents (small confession: I'm making assumptions here since I don't know any of them well), but with the exception of me, they're all conscripts. Not one wanted to be in a physical contest with individuals from the St. Martin's team, who, as I have observed before, were built like the proverbial public toilets constructed entirely from brick.

How did I know this? Firstly, by the terrified expressions on my teammates' faces. They wore the look of escaped convicts toiling through a swamp and hearing the baying of guard dogs in the distance. Secondly, they avoided any kind of physical contact throughout the first half. They weren't even keen on being *close* to a St. Martin's player. If there had been tables on the pitch, they would have jumped onto them and shrieked. As it was, they simply parted before the first St. Martin's attack. There were muttered cries of "Sorry, am I in your way?" and one of my defenders even produced a red carpet for the opposition to pound along. I exaggerate only slightly. In consequence, I found four St. Martin's attackers bearing down on me. Think of a herd of elephants charging a mouse, and you'll get the idea.

Now, I don't want to give the impression I was brave and my teammates were cowards. But I had one huge advantage over them. Motivation. I channeled Andrew's words. Destry Camberwick was standing behind me in the goal: pure, innocent, and beautiful. They were going to kick the ball into her face. *I am the keeper of her face*, I said to myself. *She will not suffer. I WILL NOT LET HER SUFFER.* It's possible I gave a banshee scream. I rushed off my line and flung myself at the ball, gathering it from the toe of the forward and into my stomach, holding on for dear life. The forward tripped over my body, raking his studs along the side of my face as he did so, and crashed into the goalpost.

The post was fine, the forward not quite so. He had to be carried off and they almost needed a crane. Thirty seconds gone and I'd already got rid of one of them. Even though I'm not very good at math, I was able to calculate that I could reduce their team to zero in about five minutes if I kept this up. This would result in my team having eleven players against none. Even Milltown could score one goal against no opposition in eighty-five minutes.

Couldn't it?

Unfortunately, I hadn't known about substitutions. We didn't have substitutes. St. Martin's had ten lined up, all of whom looked like they'd sacrifice their own mothers to get onto the pitch. One promptly took off his tracksuit (a tracksuit!) and warmed up along the touchline. Luckily, no sacrifices took place, as far as I could tell.

I tipped the ball over the bar, around the posts. I flung myself hither and yon. I saved a penalty. Andrew later said that for large parts of the first half, many on my team sat down and left me to it. A few checked their phones and caught up on Facebook and Twitter.

We almost reached halftime without conceding a goal, but a few minutes before the break, St. Martin's got a corner. Their winger swung the ball in toward the penalty spot, and I came to collect it. I timed my jump well and the ball was nearly in my grasp when all the lights went out. When I came to, I was flat on my back and the ball was in the net. Mr. Broadbent's face loomed above me, which was kinda scary because I wasn't expecting it. To be honest it's a bit scary at the best of times.

"You all right, Rob?" he said. I grunted and he stuck an ice-cold sponge into my face, which I also wasn't expecting. "That was a clear foul," he muttered. "That kid led with his elbow and smacked you right in the face. Should've been sent off. Instead we're one goal down. Can you get to your feet?"

I did, but only because he brandished the ice-cold sponge

in his right hand like a man prepared to use it. I staggered a little, but luckily the referee blew his whistle for halftime, so I sat down again. The rest of the team joined me. From what I could see through my one good eye (the other was closing rapidly), they were remarkably fresh and clean. I resembled a small mudslide.

Mr. Broadbent cleared his throat for his halftime motivational speech.

"You're all useless dropkicks," he said.

Not the most motivational of starts, in my humble opinion.

"Fight, guys. Fight," he continued. "Take a page from Rob's book. Some of you haven't broken sweat, and look at Rob's face. Look at it. It's shocking. It's disgustingly bloody and battered . . ."

I didn't like the sound of that. I almost asked him to keep quiet and hit me with the sponge again. But his words faded away. I was tired. I was so, so tired.

It's probably wise to draw a veil over the second half. We lost four–nil, even though the rest of the team *did* actually start to fight. Maybe Mr. Broadbent knew something about motivation after all. The trouble was, the St. Martin's players were fit and we weren't. We ran out of the little steam we had and were no more than walking wounded in the last ten minutes of the match—the ten minutes when they added those extra three goals.

St. Martin's was thrilled. For large parts of the game they weren't much better than us lowly Milltownians, at least as far as the scoreline was concerned. So once they beat us, all was right with the world again. They went back to their Olympic swimming pool, their sports stadium, and their digital entertainment center, knowing that the social order was reassuringly intact.

But we'd experienced pride. We'd given it our best, and losing only four-nil felt . . . well, to be honest, it felt like victory.

It was just a pity Destry Camberwick wasn't there to share it. She got sick ten minutes before kickoff and apparently her mother came and took her home. I would've laughed, but my face was too battered and bruised and painful.

24

A WEEK AFTER THE GAME AGAINST ST. MARTIN'S, I
received another anonymous text message.

> Rob, you were brilliant in the soccer match.
> But even now, you don't fully understand
> how talented you are and how everyone will
> love you, given the chance. Confidence is
> the key to defeating your shyness.
>
> I have a series of challenges. One at a time.
> What do you say? Are you willing to prove
> yourself worthy of Destry Camberwick?
> More importantly, are you willing, finally, to
> like and value yourself? Text me Y or N.

I called the number but it rang out, not even going to

voice mail. I texted again. Who are you? Nothing.

I'm imaginative. I believe this has already been touched on. So the first thing I thought about was the possibility of a stalker—someone who followed me home, maybe in a dark overcoat and a four-wheel-drive with tinted windows. But I'm also logical. Surely I'd have noticed someone following me, and besides, a stalker couldn't realistically have access to information like my phone number. No. This was someone who knew me well; they were aware of my obsession with Destry Camberwick and they also knew about the soccer game. In fact, the implication was that they'd been among the spectators.

Call me Sherlock if you will, but it took little time to draw up a list of suspects and the evidence for and against each of them.

Andrew. Evidence for: has my number (obviously) and is completely up-to-date with the state of my heart. Was definitely at the game. Evidence against: entirely unlike him. He has no problem telling me stuff to my face—cloak-and-dagger routines are not his style. Plus, the language used in the text is nothing like his normal way of writing or talking. Plus-plus, the text is an imaginative form of engagement and he is not very imaginative. Chance of mysterious communicator therefore being him? Six out of ten, tops.

Grandad. Evidence for: also knows all about the game (was there) and my love interest. Can be sneaky and surprising. He was the one who suggested the soccer game, so he has a history of interference. Evidence against: has as much chance of working a cell phone as winning gold in the hundred-meter hurdles at the next Olympics. Unless he has an accomplice? (The phone, I mean. Not the Olympics— that makes no sense at all.) The clincher: not one swear-word in the entire message. Grandad swears like other people breathe. Chance of mysterious communicator therefore being him? Two out of ten.

Mum and Dad (let's lump them together; according to Dad they're basically one person anyway). Evidence for: again, they know all about me. Weren't at the game but got full report from me and Grandad. Both know my phone number. Mum is sneaky. (I still have this feeling she tricked me into playing the soccer match while appearing to be totally against it. Mothers can *never* be trusted. If I could afford it, I'd have that inscribed on a sign and hang it on my bedroom door.) Evidence against: a strange way for parents to behave (though, to be fair, parents have a habit of being consistently *weird*); would require them buying another phone, which seems nuts (applies to Andrew, too). Not one mention of golf, which rules Dad out (see above re: Grandad and swearing). Chance of mysterious communicator therefore being them? Mum, six out of ten. Dad, zero out of ten.

Everyone else: not a chance, on the grounds that no one knows me because I'm painfully shy. It has to be one of the above. Trouble is, which one? Unless . . .

I had another suspect.

What if this came from Destry Camberwick herself? What if Andrew had told her about my feelings? It would explain why her number wasn't recognized by my phone. Other evidence for? Well, none really. In fact, her number not being recognized means she has this in common with ninety-nine point nine nine recurring percent of the world's population. I have three numbers in my phone: Andrew, Mum, and Dad. And Dad never contacts me. Evidence against? Everything. Chance of mysterious communicator therefore being her? Ten out of ten or zero out of ten, depending how emotionally invested you are in the answer.

I would not play this game. I would not reply. I would be strong. I would be patient.

I'm great at making resolutions. Keeping them is another matter.

25

I WENT TO THE PARK WITH TRIXIE, THE FLUFFY BUNDLE
of rubbish, aka FBR, the next day. It's not that I wanted to talk
to Destry again. Well, I did, but my comment about killing
her dog must have blown any chance of us having a friendly
conversation.

I just wanted to see her. In fact, I *needed* to see her.

And Trixie needed a walk. A few poos as well, it turned out.

I sat on a bench underneath a spreading tree and kept a
firm grip on Trixie's leash as she tried to get in the face of
every dog within a hundred yards. I confess I was tempted
to let her have a go a few times. Would she really attack, or
would she look at me as if I had crushed her self-esteem? It
wasn't worth finding out.

Destry came around the corner, and the world dimmed
at the edges, brightened in the center. I watched, jaw droop-
ing, until she turned another corner and disappeared from

sight. The world undimmed; my jaw undrooped.

I know I'm sounding desperate and pathetic, but I was prepared to do almost anything to see if there was a future for us. Anyway, I've made my peace with being desperate and pathetic.

I pulled out my phone, brought up my last message, and tapped reply. I typed in Y and then pressed send. Almost immediately, I got a reply.

Wise decision. I'll give you your first challenge tonight.

I rushed to the corner. I'd had a eureka moment. What if I saw Destry putting her phone back into her pocket, smiling as she realized I'd swallowed her bait?

Didn't happen.

She'd let her dog off its leash and was throwing a ball for it. The hound bounded along while pedestrians dived into bushes and other dogs tried to climb trees.

A phone didn't figure in any of this.

"I'm vegetarian," I said to Mum. "I told you yesterday."

"Yeah," said Mum, "but I didn't think you were serious."

"You thought 'I'm vegetarian' was my attempt at humor? I should enter the Melbourne Comedy Festival with material like that."

Mum turned from the stove and regarded me, her hand

on a hip. Unfortunately, the hand still gripped a ladle, which dripped chicken casserole onto the floor. I would have pointed this out but I was pinned by those eyes, which were flinty.

"Do not be a smart aleck with me, Rob," she said. "You're *not* too old to go over my knee, you know."

"Sorry, Mum," I said. I was, too. It wasn't like me to be sarcastic. "But, actually . . . I *am* too old to go over your knee."

"I know," said Mum. "Pity. Not that you were ever smacked."

"True. But the emotional torture you inflicted . . ."

"Ha, ha," said Mum. "Oh, now look." She'd noticed the dripping ladle. I pulled some paper towels from the cupboard and started to mop up. "So you don't want chicken casserole, then?" she said.

"No. Sorry. It's not vegetarian."

"But chicken is a white meat. It's not like beef."

"Mum, that does not qualify it as a vegetable. Those things that go 'cluck' around farmyards are not vegetables."

"What about fish?"

"That's different. Everyone knows fish are vegetables in the same family as carrots."

Mum did the thing with the hand on the hip again, but this time she'd put the ladle down.

"Sorry, Mum," I said again. "Honestly. But I have become a vegetarian and that means I'm no longer eating meat, white, red, or any other color. I won't eat fish. I won't eat anything that's been alive."

"Carrots were alive. Potatoes were alive."

"They don't scream when you pull them from the ground."

"Maybe they do, but you just can't hear them."

"Mum!" I put my hand on my hip but it didn't have the same effect as when she does it. "If you love animals called pets, why do you eat animals called dinner?"

"That's clever," said Mum. "Did you make that up?"

"I wish."

"For the record, by the way, I have never eaten a dog or a cat." Mum raised both hands, palms out. "But, okay. Okay. No chicken casserole for you. Though, I'm not sure what you can have for dinner."

"I'll see to myself," I said. "Most times it should be okay. If you and Dad are having chops, for example, I'll just have the potatoes and the other veg. Maybe I could get some Quorn burgers from the supermarket. Grandad said they do some good vegetarian options now."

"I might have known Pop would be behind this. He's converted you."

"It's not a religion, Mum, and he's not radicalizing me."

"But why become a vegetarian now, Rob?"

I explained I'd been reading up on the subject, that meat production was destroying the planet and was responsible for much poverty and hunger in third world countries. I also talked about animal cruelty, not just in meat production but in testing things like cosmetics. "Unnecessary suffering, Mum," I said. "We don't tolerate it in human beings. Why should we think it's okay for animals? And don't get me started on trophy hunting . . ."

"I respect your views, Rob," said Mum. "Though, to be honest, I also believe many people *do* tolerate unnecessary suffering in other people. In fact, they often go out of their way to inflict it. Read the news, watch the television any day . . ."

Becoming a vegetarian was the best decision I'd made in my admittedly short life. Not only was I making a small contribution to the welfare of the world, but I was having a serious and mature conversation with my mother about important matters. If I'd had that sign about mothers on my bedroom door, I'd consider taking it down. But I didn't, so I didn't.

"This'll be ready in ten minutes," said Mum, pointing to the pot. "So you might want to start heating up some soup or whatever."

"Soup's good," I said. "What have we got?"

"There's a nice chicken one in the cupboard."

I still don't know if she was joking.

26

I CALLED THE MYSTERY NUMBER OVER DINNER, WHEN
I took my bowl to the sink and while Mum and Dad finished their casserole. I didn't expect the call to be answered, but I wanted to keep an ear out for ringing somewhere in the house.

Nothing. I even went close to their bedroom door, but I didn't hear anything. Of course, the phone might have been on silent, so it didn't prove anything. For some reason I didn't want to tell Mum and Dad about it either. I know I should have. It's parents' business when you're getting messages from a stranger, but so far there was nothing creepy in the texts themselves. I vowed I would tell them soon, and certainly if I received anything weird.

But for the time being this was a mystery, and I like mysteries.

* * *

The message came through at 10:10 p.m. Was the person responsible deliberately making it late so I couldn't check out possible senders? If it had come through during dinner, I could've eliminated Mum and Dad, thereby trimming my suspect list to two. It didn't matter, I guessed. I opened the message.

**Good evening, Rob. Your first
challenge follows, but I want to tell
you why this challenge and the ones
to come are worthy of your time.
You are in love and that's wonderful.
Maybe it won't last, but maybe it will.
Who can say? What I do know is this:
How can anyone else love you if YOU
don't think you're worth anything?**

**So these challenges are not about
impressing Destry Camberwick. They
are about Rob Fitzgerald impressing
Rob Fitzgerald. Remember this.**

**Challenge 1. You will enter the
Milltown's Got Talent competition,
which is scheduled for two weeks
from Friday. This gives you time to
polish your act and find ways to**

**overcome panic attacks. I would
wish you luck, but the point of this
challenge is that you don't need it.**

I closed my phone and then closed my eyes.
A public performance. Probably my worst nightmare.

27

___

I TOOK ANDREW INTO MY CONFIDENCE. THOUGH I LIKE trying to figure things out by myself, I also desperately needed advice. Plus, if Andrew *was* behind this, I'd be able to tell from his reaction when I showed him the texts. You see, Andrew is not a good actor. He's sometimes forced to read parts when we're doing drama in English, and to call him "wooden" would be an insult to trees. So if he had any part in this, he wouldn't be able to hide it.

He was stunned. And strangely excited.

"This is *so* cool," he said as he read through the text thread. "A real mystery. Who's behind it, do ya think?"

I ran through my short list of suspects and my reasoning.

"Yeah, well, you're right it's not me," he said. "I couldn't write this sort of stuff in an essay, let alone a text message."

"Just because you always write the letter u instead of the

word doesn't mean you couldn't compose something accurate if you wanted."

"Yeah, maybe. But this isn't my style, man, and you know it."

I did.

"So your grandad's the prime suspect, then?" he said after I'd explained how I didn't think this was something Mum and Dad would do. They'd spent their entire lives protecting me from stressful situations. It just didn't seem in character. Having said that, Mum appeared to use a sneaky form of reverse psychology regarding my goalkeeping debut . . .

"Pop can't operate an electric kettle," I pointed out. "And I've never seen him near a computer or a phone. I dunno. It seems unlikely."

"But who else? As you pointed out, you're not exactly having to fight off a legion of friends."

Fight off a legion of friends? That was sophisticated language. I tried to stop thinking about it. You can go crazy suspecting everyone.

"How about someone else that either you or Mum or Pop have mentioned this whole love business to?" I replied. "Someone who's watching but keeping a distance. A mole, an infiltrator. Like you were doing with Destry Camberwick on my behalf. Getting the lowdown, while I remain hidden. Any more progress, by the way?"

"Oh, yeah. She's cool, from what I can see. Loves her dog, as you know. No idea about her musical tastes, but I'll get around to that. Doesn't seem to have any particular hobbies, but goes to the movies occasionally. She likes 'sincerity,' it seems." Andrew made quotation marks in the air with his fingers. "Told me she hates phonies. Nothing that useful so far, but I can't be too pushy."

I nodded just as the bell went for the end of recess. Andrew handed my phone back.

"And by the way," he said. "I haven't mentioned you and Destry Camberwick to anyone. I wouldn't do that." He tapped the casing of my phone. "So are you going to do this?"

"I don't think I *can* do this," I said. It was true. I had explained about panic attacks to people before, but I'd learned that unless someone experienced an attack of their own, they had little idea what it was like. It seems simple to them. *But all you have to do is breathe deeply*, they'd say. *Stay calm. Imagine the audience is sitting on the toilet. Get some backbone. Be a man.* They don't understand that sometimes your muscles lock up, your heart pounds, you suddenly lose control over parts of your body. You vomit. You're overcome with a terror so vivid that all you can do is cover your head with your hands and hope to die. It can last all day, even when the worst is over.

They don't understand.

Daniel Smith caught up with me at lunchtime.

"Wanna fight, Fitzgerald?" he said. "Whaddya say? Cat got yer tongue? Huh? Wanna fight? C'mon. Be a man."

"A word in your shell-like ear, Mr. Smith," said Miss Pritchett, drawing him away. It was clear to me, beyond a shadow of a doubt, that Miss Pritchett lived in a world, possibly another universe, the rest of us were unaware of, and she possessed powers beyond the dreams of mortals.

I entered my name on the Milltown's Got Talent sign-up form, tacked on the wall next to main reception.

I could always cross it out later.

28

"WHAT THE BLANKETY HELL IS MILLTOWN'S GOT TALENT?"
said Grandad.

"Have you ever seen *Australia's Got Talent*?" I replied.

"Nope," said Pop. "And I've been in Australia for a hundred and fifteen years so far and never seen any evidence of talent anywhere. Why? Has it finally made an appearance?"

"It's a television show, Pop," I said. The thing is, with Grandad, you can never be sure if he's pulling your leg or not. He has a strange sense of humor. I called it "dry" once. *I'm so dry*, he replied, *I need peeing on*. There was, therefore, no point in checking his reaction to the news that I'd signed up for the talent show. I suspect he *is* a good actor, and if he was the face behind the text messages, I wouldn't find out by trying to trip him up so obviously.

"Ah, television," said Pop. "The blankety glass-fronted teat we all suck on for comfort. Or does it suck on *us*, young Rob?

Does it drain us of wonder and passion and vitality?" The word "suck" obviously inspired him because he did it with his teeth and this set off the whistling, which was a shame because he'd sounded really intelligent up to that point. "Rarely watch it," he added. "Very rarely. So tell me all."

"It's an amateur talent show, Pop, but you get to do your thing in front of millions. People sign up—all kinds of people, singers, dancers, comedians, jugglers, magicians, you name it. And they perform in front of a panel of celebrity judges. The overall winner is normally voted in by the television audience."

"Sounds appalling," said Pop. "And this passes for entertainment, does it?"

"It seems so."

"And Milltown's Got Talent is presumably your school's version of this, where revolting young people thrash electric guitars and gyrate onstage while blankety wailing?"

I tried to find a flaw in Grandad's description, but it was fairly close to the truth.

"Pretty much," I said.

"And you've decided to do an act in front of the entire school?"

"Not *decided*, exactly," I said. "I'm keeping my options open."

"You don't play guitar," Grandad pointed out. "I'm assuming you're not expert at gyrating but I'm guessing you can wail. Is that what you're thinking of doing?"

"I can't sing, Pop," I said, "and it's true I don't play a musical instrument. But the talent show can be about anything. Maybe you could show me a few of your magic tricks . . ."

Pop is a good magician. He can make pens and stuff disappear and then pull whatever it is out from behind your ear, that sort of thing. Some of his card tricks and illusions are really impressive.

"I could, young Rob . . ." Grandad scratched at his whiskery chin. "I could. But when is this show?"

"Two weeks away."

"Ah. No way, then. The tricks I *could* teach you; there's nothing special about them and you can probably track them down on your computer anyway. Isn't that one of the functions of those blankety things, to remove all mystery from the world?" (It was a rhetorical question, because he continued without a pause. Nonetheless, I'd think about these words later and wonder again whether Grandad was behind the texts.) "The problem is time. Even the simplest trick takes weeks and weeks of practice. Some of the best ones, the ones worth watching and therefore worth performing, can take *years* of practice. A bad magic show is a blankety dreadful experience. You'd be better off singing a song badly."

I gazed out of the window while I mulled over his words. A light rain was falling and the world seemed slightly dispirited.

"What about your panic attacks?" said Pop.

"A good question," I said. "And, yes. If I decide to go

ahead with this, then I'll be terrified about having one in front of strangers. But someone once said, 'do not fear fear. Its only purpose is to let you know that something is worth doing.'" I kept a close eye on Grandad's expression. "What do you think of that?"

There was a long pause.

"Sounds like a steaming pile of blankety poop," said Pop eventually.

He didn't use the word "poop," by the way.

29

I WAS WORKING ON A PARTICULARLY TRICKY MATH
problem (it needed *way* more than taking my shoes and
socks off—I'm not sure if even the entire class's bared toes
would have helped me with this one) when I was tapped on
the shoulder by Ms. Singh, the math teacher. She bent down
and whispered in my ear.

"Rob, Mr. Broadbent wants to see you now in the gym.
He says it won't take long, so you can leave your bag here."

I scuttled off to the gym. Well, I didn't exactly *scuttle*. It
was more of an amble. There were still thirty minutes left in
the lesson and I wasn't keen to get back to the math problem, which, frankly, seemed impossible. Then again, all
math problems appear impossible. Maybe they are. Maybe
it's all an elaborate hoax designed to make students' lives
miserable.

Mr. Broadbent was shouting at a bunch of kids racing

around the basketball court, making strange squeaky noises with their sneakers and sweating profusely. I've often wondered what makes people train to be PE teachers. Is it a genuine fondness for the smell of sweat? I have no idea. It's like a math problem. Mr. B spotted me and blew his whistle.

"Okay, guys," he said. "Warming-down routines. You know the drill."

I sat on the bench and watched the class warm down. Mr. Broadbent sat at my side.

"Hi, Rob," he said. "How are you feeling after your exertions on the soccer pitch?"

"Good," I lied. In fact, I still had the bruises, though the nightmares were beginning to fade. I was a little suspicious of his question. If I said I was still in pain, was he going to smack me in the face with an ice-cold sponge again? It was something he appeared to enjoy.

"I've got exciting news," he said.

I waited. Most adults' exciting news isn't exciting. It's often not even news.

"There was a scout at the game," Mr. Broadbent continued. "Someone from the state under-sixteen squad. I actually think he came to see members of the St. Martin's team, but it seems he left with only one name on his lips. Yours. He called me half an hour ago."

This was probably incredibly exciting for a PE teacher, though it wasn't too much of a struggle for me to hide my enthusiasm.

"The state under-sixteen squad," I said. I had to say something.

"Yup. He wants you to try out." Mr. Broadbent held up a hand as if to stop me from blubbering and dribbling with overexcitement. "Doesn't mean you'll get selected for the team, you understand. No guarantees. But it's a fabulous opportunity."

I held up my own hand. "Mr. Broadbent," I said. "You've obviously mistaken me for someone who gives a poo poo. Let me tell you something. I don't like sports. I hate soccer. I only played in that game to impress Destry Camberwick, who wasn't impressed because she wasn't there. This makes me a complete and utter fool. I nearly lost an eye and a couple of limbs. I flirted with brain damage, and all for nothing. If you think I'm ever going to go on a soccer pitch again, then you are delusional. Please tell this scout to insert his offer where the sun is unlikely to ever shine."

Actually, I didn't say any of that. I made it all up later.

"Oh?" I replied, which, to be honest, isn't quite as witty.

"Yes," he continued. "You'd go for training with the rest of the squad, and there's a distinct chance you'll be part of the interstate soccer tournament taking place in Brisbane next winter."

"Brisbane?" I said. I didn't want to give the impression that "Oh" was my only conversational gambit.

"Yes. Isn't that great? All expenses paid. And, who knows, it may be the start of a tremendous career." His eyes were shining. For a moment I thought he might blubber and dribble with overexcitement. "As far as I know, no one from Milltown has ever been offered anything like this. What do you say?"

I looked at the basketball guys warming down but found nothing in the way of inspiration.

"I'll think about it," I said finally.

"Of course," said Mr. Broadbent. "I'm happy to meet with your parents and we can talk it over. But you can't think about it too long. This is a once-in-a-lifetime opportunity and you need to grab it with both hands. Come with me to the office and I'll print out the state enrollment forms for you."

I trailed behind him to his office. Every second counts when it comes to putting off math problems.

30

"OKAY," SAID ANDREW. "LET ME SUMMARIZE YOUR argument so far."

We'd gone back to his place after school. I hadn't mentioned the state soccer squad offer to him because I was doing my best to forget it.

"You're thinking about performing in the Milltown's Got Talent competition because your mystery texter suggested it, and for some reason you think it's a good idea to follow his or her suggestions . . ."

"It's not so much—"

Andrew held up a hand. This was happening often lately.

"Shush," he said. "I'm thinking, and that's a delicate matter at the best of times. If you talk, I'll lose my thread and go and play video games instead."

I shushed.

"But your problem," he continued, "is that you get panic

attacks when you're the center of attention, so you want to perform an act in front of the whole school in such a way that no one notices you. Is that right?"

There was a long pause.

"You can talk now, Rob," he said. "I have control."

"Basically, yes," I said.

"Okay. Here's what we do. I get up onstage and introduce you. I say, 'Please welcome Rob Fitzgerald, the Invisible Man' and that's it. Two minutes of no one on the stage—you can hide in the toilets if it suits—and then . . . thunderous applause."

"'doctor, the Invisible Man's outside.' 'Tell him I can't see him!'"

"Is that a joke?"

"Kind of."

"Okay, so that's ruled out the stand-up comedy routine."

"I've got other jokes. Knock-knock ones, mainly."

Andrew held up his hand again. What is it with raised hands? "And I'd be grateful if you'd keep them to yourself. No, it's a tricky one, Rob. As far as I can tell, you have no talents whatsoever."

"Hey, cut it out. I don't come to you for insults." It was true. Grandad normally supplied those and he was very good.

"You can't sing, you can't play a musical instrument, and you can't tell jokes. What about dancing?"

"Well . . ."

"Here." Andrew pulled out his phone and pressed a couple of icons, and dance music spilled out at surprising volume. "Dance for me."

"What, now?"

"Yes, now."

So I did. I'm rather proud of my dancing. There's a full-length mirror in my bedroom and I sometimes dance in front of it. It may seem immodest, but I think I'm very innovative in my dance techniques. I do moves (please note that I *never* bust them) that no one else has ever tried, interpreting music in new and exciting ways. After thirty seconds, Andrew switched off his phone.

"Okay, you can't dance, either."

"Wait a moment . . ."

"Trust me, Rob." Andrew got up and paced the room, his hands on either side of his head, fingers against temples. "Think, Andrew," he said in a low voice. "There has to be something that Rob can do. You've been friends for ages. Surely, you must have detected *some* talent, no matter how carefully hidden?"

"Hey," I said, but he ignored me.

"Soccer, true, but you can't enact a soccer game onstage." He clicked his fingers and wheeled around to face me.

"That dog you walk. Does it do tricks?"

"You mean Trixie."

"Trixie the Tricksy Dog. Perfect. Didn't an act like that win *Australia's Got Talent* one year? Some woman and her

dog that could do amazing things. Somersaults, baking a
cake, performing quadratic equations, and singing a med-
ley from *The Sound of Music*? All at the same time."

"I don't think so. Anyway, Trixie doesn't do tricks, as far
as I know. Unless you count pooing twice your body weight
in one go as a good trick."

"Frankly," said Andrew, "I'd pay good money to see that
on the Milltown High stage, but I don't think it'll work.
Unless it does it on command?"

I shook my head.

"Pity," he said.

"Look," I said. "Let's just give up. You're right. I have no
talent, and anyway, it's crazy to think I could control my
panic attacks long enough to get through an act. It terrifies
me just thinking about it. I have to accept my limitations.
I'm useless—"

"GOT IT!" yelled Andrew. He rushed over and punched
me hard on my arm. It's his way of showing affection, and I
wish he wouldn't.

"Ow," I said. "What have you got?"

"The act you'll do in Milltown's Got Talent. It's something you already do really well, according to you. And it's
perfect because it won't be like Rob Fitzgerald will be up
onstage at all, so you shouldn't have a panic attack. It's woe-
ful, true, and everyone will hate it, but that's not the point,
is it? The point is, it'll achieve the first challenge. Call me a
genius, mate. Call me a genius."

"You're a genius."

"I know."

"So are you going to tell me this amazing plan whereby I'll be up onstage and *not* up onstage at the same time?"

He did.

"You're a genius," I said.

"I know," he said.

31

GRANDAD COMES TO OUR HOUSE FOR LUNCH ONCE A week, on Sunday. Dad picks him up and drops him home again. Pop doesn't stay long. According to Mum it's because he's independent. According to Pop it's because he doesn't like us.

This time, two of us passed on the roast beef. Grandad has been vegetarian for as long as I can remember, but I've never asked him about it. It's just the way it is, a peculiarity that isn't really a peculiarity because I'm used to it.

Mum placed a burger on my plate and one on Grandad's.

"What's this?" he said, poking it with his fork as one might poke a body to discern if it's still alive. The burger didn't twitch.

"Bean burger," said Mum.

"I don't care what it's been. What is it now?" said Pop.

"Very funny, Dad," said Dad. "It was funny the first time

I heard it, back in 1987, and you have to say that, as a joke, it's aged well."

"I wish I could say the same for you, you blankety heap of dog vomit," said Grandad.

"I know which act I'm doing for Milltown's Got Talent," I said. I wasn't trying to stop an argument. Sunday dinners are always like this and everyone seems to have fun. It stopped the conversation, though.

"I'm sorry, Rob," said Mum. "What's Milltown's Got Talent?"

I explained. I felt slightly bad that I'd taken Grandad into my confidence but not my parents. In my defense, I hadn't made any decisions to actually do it—in fact, the odds were overwhelmingly against. Mum and Dad listened and didn't say anything, but I could read their expressions. *What about panic attacks? Rob has difficulty talking to the search assistant on a computer* . . .

"The beauty of this act is that it won't be me doing it. Well, it will, but in some ways, if I can get my headspace right, it won't. Even though it will be *me* onstage, it won't *be* me doing it . . ."

"That's it," said Grandad. "Rob's finally cracked. Alan, you call the ambulance while I fashion a straitjacket from a pair of curtains. . . ."

"Can I perform the act after dinner?" I said. "I need to get as much practice in as possible and I want your honest criticism."

"Of course," said Dad. "And you can rely on your grand-father to be honest. And critical. Unfortunately."

I set up the front room while Mum and Dad loaded the dishwasher. Grandad helped me. Well, I say "helped," but basically it was drawing the curtains. I moved the furniture back against the walls so there was a round space in which I could perform.

"Are you sure this is a good idea, Rob?" said Grandad while I was doing this. "Don't get me wrong. I think it's brilliant if you can stand up in front of people and perform, but . . ."

"But you worry I won't be able to."

"I worry you'll try, get a panic attack in front of the entire school, and freeze. Not the end of the world, true, but you aren't full of confidence now, and I'd hate to see you hurt."

"Ah, Pop," I said. "That's so sweet. You really care about me."

"No need to exaggerate," said Pop. "I'd find it embarrass-ing, that's all. You're family, even though I will deny that in a court of law if you ever claim I said it."

"I have to try, Grandad," I said. "That's all I'm doing now. Just trying."

"Well, I'm proud of you," said Grandad, "though I will deny—"

"I won't quote you," I said.

Mum and Dad came in and sat in the chairs against the wall. Pop sat on the couch. I stood to the side and briefly gazed at my audience of three.

"I need to give you context," I said.

"You need to give me dessert," said Grandad.

"Shhh," said Mum and Dad together.

"Lady Macbeth," I said, "has just persuaded her husband, Macbeth, to kill the Scottish king, Duncan, who has come to stay at the Macbeth house overnight . . ."

"It's one reason I never stay over here," said Grandad.

"Will you shut up?" said Mum. She turned to me. "So that's the plan. Acting out a scene from Shakespeare."

"It's why I said it would be me, but *not* me," I replied. "If I can get into character, then it will be someone else up there— in this case, Macbeth himself. I will be hiding beneath him."

"But what about putting it into context? Like you're doing now," said Dad. "You aren't hiding now."

"True," I said. "But I won't be putting it into context in the show. I'll just be acting the scene. Maybe my English teacher can provide the context, or maybe it's not impor- tant. I just thought you guys should know."

"Okay," said Pop. "So this Macbeth person is going to kill the king. Is this after dessert?"

"Shut up," said Mum and Dad.

"It is, actually," I said. "They've had a banquet and the king's gone to bed. So Macbeth is trying to pluck up the courage to do it. Are you with me?"

My audience nodded. Every single one of them.

I took a deep breath and stepped out into my homemade theater-in-the-round.

32

OKAY. ATTEMPT NUMBER FORTY-TWO AT THE DESTRY
poem. The previous forty-one have been consigned to the
garbage bin, where they rot, along with assorted fish heads
and broccoli stalks.

I suspect my poems stink more than the decaying food.

I'm reluctant to give up rhyme, though so far the ones
I've chosen verge on the desperate. (For example, I just realized that "Destry" and "broccoli" might go together. *Destry
in the vestry, as sweet and tasty as broccoli.* I know. The smell
makes you gag; maggots are gathering around my pen.)

Rhyme can be tricky, but that doesn't mean you can't be
sneaky with it. There's no reason to simply use end-stopped
lines all the time. What about enjambement (when one
line flows on to the other)? Or half rhymes? No one would
argue that these aren't respectable literary techniques. I feel
inspired.

She seared my vision, this angel called Destry,
And I knew she was the best she
Could be. Her last name, Camberwick,
Was magic, a miracle, a wondrous trick
Of sound. I was totally smitten,
A love-lost kid, a freaked-out kitten . . .

Forgive me while I bang my head against the wall until
it hurts.

My head, not the wall.

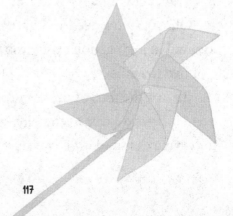

33

I CROUCHED A LITTLE, LOOKED OVER MY SHOULDER, AND took a tentative step toward my audience. I froze, my gaze fixed somewhere above their heads, a look of fear (hopefully) plastered across my face. Slowly, slowly, I stretched out one arm.

"Brilliant," said Grandad. "Let's have dessert."

"Oh, for Pete's sake," yelled Mum. "You're like a small child, Pat. Have some respect. Rob is acting, and all you can do is make stupid jokes."

"Yeah, act your age," said Dad.

"Oh, you guys need to lighten up," said Grandad. "Rob knows I'm joking, don't you, Rob?"

I had to smile.

"It's just the four of us," Pop continued. "I wouldn't have done it if we'd been in the blankety Sydney Opera House, for crying out loud. Rob can start again."

"And will you shut up this time?" said Mum.

Grandad pulled an imaginary zipper across his lips.

I did the whole crouch, backward glance, step, freeze, and arm stretch routine once again. "Is this a dagger which I see before me," I hissed. "The handle toward my hand? Come, let me clutch thee." I closed my hand over empty air and started back a step or two. "I have thee not, and yet I see thee still. Art thou not, fatal vision, sensible to feeling as to sight? Or art thou but a dagger of the mind, a false creation, proceeding from the heat-oppressed brain? I see thee yet, in form as palpable as this which now I draw."

I stepped out of character for a moment. "I'll have a dagger in my belt when I do the actual show," I explained. "A plastic one because I suspect Milltown wouldn't be too happy if I brought a real one to school." That was something of an understatement. They'd probably judge a lunchtime detention a serious underreaction for threatening the whole school with a blade. "Are you with me so far?" I said.

"Absolutely," said Mum.

"Lay on, Macduff," said Grandad. He spread his arms out as Mum and Dad turned toward him. "What did I say? Rob asked."

I took up where I'd left off.

"Thou marshall'st me the way that I was going; and such an instrument I was to use. Mine eyes are made the fools o' the other senses, or else worth all the rest." I gave a small scream of terror. "I see thee still, and on thy blade and dud-geon gouts of blood, which was not so before." I shook my head. "There's no such thing: it is the bloody business which informs thus to mine eyes."

I straightened and looked around me, one hand out-stretched. This was the hand that was going to hold the plastic dagger. I wished I'd thought of it before, because I felt a bit of a jerk, but I wasn't going to stop now and get one from the kitchen. Grandad would almost certainly ask me to bring him back a piece of cake.

"Now," I said, "o'er the one halfworld nature seems dead, and wicked dreams abuse the curtain'd sleep; witchcraft celebrates pale Hecate's offerings, and wither'd murder, alarum'd by his sentinel, the wolf, whose howl's his watch, thus with his stealthy pace. With Tarquin's ravishing strides, towards his design moves like a ghost." I looked down at my feet. "Thou sure and firm-set earth, hear not my steps, which way they walk, for fear thy very stones prate of my whereabout, and take the present horror from the time, which now suits with it." I gave a hollow laugh, one (I hoped) full of anguish and self-loathing. "Whiles I threat, he lives: words to the heat of deeds too cold breath gives."

"Ding-dong," said Grandad. Mum opened her mouth to speak, but I beat her to it. Who'd have guessed Grandad knew this play so well?

"I go, and it is done; the bell invites me. Hear it not, Duncan; for it is a knell that summons thee to heaven or to hell." I walked off between Mum's and Dad's chairs. The effect was ruined slightly because that meant I ran into the wall, but I hoped my audience would get the general idea.

There was a loud round of applause. Well, as loud as three people can generate. It sounded genuine, as well.

34

AFTER WE'D DROPPED GRANDAD OFF, DAD AND I WENT
to the golf course. We normally go in the morning, but Dad
had been busy so he'd decided to fit in nine holes in the
afternoon.

I held the little furry hat while Dad addressed the ball on
the first hole. I didn't say anything but he still hooked the
ball (or was it sliced?).

"Bugger," he said, handing me back the hatless one wood.
I dutifully covered its head and returned it to the trolley as
we wandered off into the long grass.

"So, how's it going with your girlfriend?" said Dad.

"Well, it's not going," I replied. "And she's not my girlfriend. In fact, she still has no idea who I am."

"Yeah, but that's bound to change after your talent competition."

"Knowing my luck, she'll get sick like she did before

the soccer game and miss it." I gave that statement some thought. "Or, knowing my luck, she *won't* get sick and will witness the whole grisly road accident." I'd been having second thoughts about the talent show. I'd been having third, fourth, and fifth thoughts, actually, and I suspected Dad was right. Destry would know who I was, all right. A spectacular bozo, an idiot in search of a village, and the undisputed laughingstock of Milltown High.

My self-esteem is not great at the best of times.

"Confidence," Dad said over his shoulder, as if reading my mind. "That's the key with women. Hey, you want any advice, just ask, okay?"

"If I want to bust moves while chatting up Destry Camberwick," I said, "you'll definitely be my first port of call, Dad."

"I'm serious," said Dad. "You may look at me and see a fat, bald, old loser . . ." He found his ball in the long grass and gazed at it, like it was the ball's fault for hiding in rough country, when it should have been nestled, like a good, obedient golf ball, in the center of the fairway. I gave him the nine iron without being asked. "Hey, Rob," he said. "Don't argue with my self-portrait, all right?"

"Dad," I said. "You are NOT a loser. Fat, bald, and old without a doubt—there's no point hiding our heads in the sand—but you are definitely *not* a loser."

Dad parted blades of grass so he could get a decent view of the ball.

"Okay, maybe a *bit* of a loser," I continued. "Not much of one, probably . . ." I fiddled with the remaining clubs in the golf bag. "Right, fair enough. I won't argue," I said. "'Fat, bald, old loser' seems to cover it."

"You're spending too much time with Grandad," said Dad as he took a practice swipe with the nine iron. "And that's a worry."

He hit the ball, and even I could see it was a great shot. The ball rose sharply and cleared the crown of surrounding trees by inches. I moved a couple of steps to my left to watch as it hit the edge of the green and rolled agonizingly close to the pin.

"Great shot, Dad," I said.

"Not always a loser, then?"

"Oh, please," I said. "Grow up."

We walked toward the green.

"I wasn't a great dancer," said Dad. "In fact, I was useless. When I look back on it, there's no reason why your mum should have given me a second glance. God, she was a looker in her day, Rob! Don't get me wrong, she's still a fine-looking woman, but . . ."

"So why did she? Give you a second glance, I mean."

Dad whistled as we reached the green. "That *was* a great shot," he said. "Almost makes up for that hook off the tee." I handed him his putter.

"I was a union organizer," he said. "I tell ya, those were the days, Rob. Strikes to improve our working conditions, addressing members, negotiating with employers, issuing media releases. Happiest days of my life when I look back on them."

"And . . . ?"

"And your mum fell in love with that enthusiasm. At least that's what she said years later when I asked why she'd gone for me. 'You believed in something and you fought for it,' she said. 'There's nothing more attractive than a passion for a cause, even if that cause is doomed. Maybe *especially* if it's doomed.'"

I watched as he lined up the putt and sank the ball. I even gave a round of applause. He raised his club as if he'd just won the US Open and waved a hand at nonexistent spectators. I took the putter and put it back into the bag.

"You're trying to tell me something, Dad," I said. "I wish you'd just do it."

He put a hand on my shoulder. "You've become vegetarian. You've bored us with the reasons why. No offense. We've heard about animal cruelty, greenhouse gas emissions, and even though I don't agree with everything you say—to be honest, Rob, I think my love of steaks overrules my conscience—there's no doubt you're passionate about it all. So . . ."

"So I should persuade Destry Camberwick that I'm passionate by letting her know I'm vegetarian."

"Oh, no," said Dad. "That's *not* what I'm saying at all. I'm saying if you feel strongly about something, then it shouldn't be kept to yourself. It should be a stamp on your personality, a definition of who you are, because if no one can tell what you believe in, then you might as well not believe in anything."

I chewed on this throughout the next hole and came to a startling and somewhat shocking conclusion. Dad was right. Trust me, it hurts to admit it. But now it seemed obvious. Trying to impress Destry with my beliefs would be as pitiful as trying to impress someone with the amount of money in your wallet. You might succeed, but, almost by definition, the person you're impressing wouldn't be worth the effort.

Being vegetarian. Supporting animal rights. Maybe it was time to stop treating it all like a shameful secret. Maybe I needed to stop feeding my low self-esteem. Maybe it was time to be myself and not worry what anyone else thought.

35

I ONLY LASTED TEN MINUTES OUTSIDE THE SCHOOL
cafeteria before I was taken to the principal. I waited outside
her office for fifteen minutes before she opened the door
and called me in. (Well, bellowed me in.) They do that on
purpose—keep you waiting, so your imagination goes
into overdrive. I've seen detective shows on television.
It's psychological manipulation, so when you're finally
confronted with your offense, you're happy—no, *eager*—to
confess. *I did it, Your Honor, so cuff me and take me down. I've
done the crime and now I'll do the time.*

"I'm disappointed in you, Rob," Miss Cunningham
roared. Or it might have been a bellow. Sometimes it's difficult to tell the difference when your ears are ringing.

I hung my head. This is something I've always done, even
when people aren't yelling at me. It's instinctive and comes
with shyness and low self-esteem. Try to make yourself

small, avoid eye contact, and perhaps people will let you go. Invisibility is the goal, even if you know it can't be achieved.

"There are many students at this school," she continued, "who I would expect to be troublesome, but I did not count you among them. Perhaps you will be so good as to explain your behavior?"

I've spent a lot of time with Grandad and, despite what Mum and Dad say, his influence hasn't been all bad. Suddenly I saw this situation from his point of view. What would Pop do if someone at the senior center called him into their office and accused him of behaving badly? He wouldn't hang his head, even if he knew he was in the wrong. If he felt himself in the right, then . . . well, hang on to your blankety hats, because blankety brown stuff would splatter blankety fans. And I *hadn't* done anything wrong. So why was I behaving as if I had? I raised my head and met Miss Cunningham's eyes. My fear had miraculously melted away.

"I haven't been troublesome, Miss Cunningham," I said. "I've been protesting."

"About our cafeteria serving meat."

"Yes."

"And did you get permission for your protest, before you stood displaying an offensive sign in front of the whole school?"

"No," I said. "I don't need permission to tell the truth. Which is what my sign did. But I know what *is* troublesome, Miss Cunningham. When a school tries to stop free speech."

Boy, that remark pressed a button. Miss Cunningham turned an interesting shade of purple, her eyes morphed into shards of granite, and her mouth became a slit. At any other time I would probably have wet my pants, but as I say, I was . . . calm.

"'Every burger you buy from this cafeteria is a nail in the world's coffin.'" Miss Cunningham's voice rose in volume, which I'd imagined was anatomically impossible. Pictures on the wall rattled. "That is a silly exaggeration, Rob. And how do you think our cafeteria staff felt? They're trying to make a living. Did you think about that when you made your childish protest?"

I hadn't, but it occurred to me that the argument was shifting from the main point. I didn't think that was fair.

"I'm not saying students shouldn't buy food from the cafeteria, Miss Cunningham," I said. "I'm asking them to think about what it means to eat meat. You say I'm exaggerating, but I'm not. Eating meat is bad for the world. Perhaps the cafeteria should sell healthy vegetarian food. That'd be good for business and good for the students. There's almost nothing vegetarian on the menu, and if the deep fryer broke down, there'd be nothing on the menu at all. Everything they sell is brown."

I could have said more, but Miss Cunningham wasn't in the mood for healthy debate. She suspended me for three days.

I think that was for arguing with her, rather than destroying the cafeteria staff's lives, but I guess it doesn't matter. I waited in the corridor while the reception staff got in touch with Grandad. He's on the emergency contact list because Mum and Dad both work. The school phoned them, too, anyway. It took Grandad half an hour to come pick me up. He's a little unsteady on his legs, even with the cane, but as he says himself, he gets to where he wants to go. Eventually.

"Young Rob," he said when he'd signed whatever needed to be signed at the front desk and I was released into his custody. "Suspended, huh?" He glanced at the sign that was propped against my knees. "You're a danger to society. Nothing more or less than a vegetarian terrorist. Excuse me a moment."

Grandad opened the door to the principal's office without knocking and walked straight in. I have no idea what he said, because he closed the door behind him and even Miss Cunningham's roar became muffled. But I guessed he was offering his frank opinion on her suitability for the job of principal. I suspect blankety words were used (and not by Miss Cunningham). As Pop once said, when you've been through a war and are close to kicking the bucket, biting the dust, cashing in your chips, going belly-up, checking out, snuffing it, and taking a dirt nap, then you really don't care about hurting people's feelings anymore.

Not that Grandad ever worried about that at the best of times.

36

"YOU ARE *NOT* STAYING AT HOME UNSUPERVISED," SAID Mum. "Playing computer games or watching television or listening to music is not, in my book, a punishment."

Mum isn't like Grandad. She believes being suspended from school is clear evidence of guilt. Even if it was a case of mistaken identity, if I could prove I was out of the country at the time of the alleged crime, she'd still support the school.

"I'm not happy with you, Rob," she said. I chopped up vegetables for dinner. I'd promised to do a vegetarian stir-fry for everyone, though Dad looked slightly less than thrilled at the prospect. "So I will drop you off at Grandad's place first thing in the morning and pick you up after work."

"You think *Grandad* is a punishment, then?" I said.

Mum folded her arms.

"I don't know what's got into you recently," she said. "I

really don't. You are turning into a smart aleck, and I never thought I'd say that. You're talking back . . ."

"I'm not talking back . . ."

"See, you're doing it now. I've read about this, when your child becomes a teenager and suddenly they change, become horrible and hateful. But I never thought you'd be like that."

I wanted to tell her that I thought she was overreacting, but figured this wouldn't cool the situation down. So I just chopped vegetables while she went on about how shameful it was to have a child suspended from school, how this was the last time it would happen, and how maybe she and Dad had been too lenient in their dealings with me. I let her words batter against me because I knew she was hurt and puzzled and worried. But I also wanted to remind her that the shy, retiring, *scared* Rob Fitzgerald might have been easy to deal with, but was basically miserable. Now I was gaining confidence—not huge amounts, it had to be said, but *some*—and I could catch glimpses of the person I might become. That made me feel . . . happy. But I also needed to remember that Mum might find the journey at least as rocky as me. Maybe rockier. And I should make allowances where I could.

"So, what do you want to do today?" said Pop. "We could catch a film or maybe go to a pub, get drunk, and pick up loose women."

I'd arrived at the old-age home at seven thirty, but Grandad had been up for two hours anyway, he told me. *It comes with age,* he'd said. *Getting up earlier and earlier and finding your bladder can't make it for half an hour throughout the night.* This was way too much information, but that's never stopped him before.

"I have strict instructions, Pop," I said. "I am to do whatever schoolwork I can. I'm not to play with my phone, watch television, or enjoy myself in any way until three forty-five, when school's officially over."

"So your mother didn't actually *forbid* getting drunk and picking up loose women?"

"I know what I want to do later, Grandad," I said.

"You want to learn how to play chess," he said.

"Do I?"

"Yes. You just don't know it yet. But I'll teach you how to play and then I'll kick your sorry backside."

"Wow," I said. "You make it sound so attractive, I couldn't possibly say no. But I know what I want to do *after* you've taught me chess and *after* you've kicked my sorry backside."

"What?"

"Take Trixie for a walk." It was true. I was becoming attached to that fluffy bundle of rubbish and it wasn't because I wanted to see Destry Camberwick. The dog had attitude, despite there being no reason for it. Maybe I had more in common with it than I'd thought.

"Blankety hell," said Grandad. "If anyone was reading a

transcript of this conversation, they'd never guess who was thirteen years old and who was the old fart." He pointed an accusing finger at me. "I want to be like you when I grow up."

Grandad taught me chess and then kicked my apologetic rear end. Twice. After that we went in search of the FBR. Agnes was happy to hand Trixie over.

"I can't walk the distances I used to," she informed me. "Don't ever get old, Rob. That's my best advice to you."

"I certainly don't intend to," said Grandad.

"You," said Agnes, "are the most pathetic and childish idiot I've ever known. And I used to work in politics," she added, "so the bar for idiocy has been set exceptionally high."

"I think she's seriously attracted to me," said Pop after we'd walked a few hundred yards. "It's not surprising. She's only human."

"She certainly hides it well, Pop," I said.

"Don't be fooled, young Rob. It's clear she thinks I'm hot. Her insults are a pathetic and frankly transparent camouflage for her true feelings. No. Anyone can see she has a thing for me." He sucked on his teeth for a few moments and I was treated to a brief whistle. "Trouble is," he added, "that thing *could* be a baseball bat."

Even though I was in deep trouble with Mum and Dad and had done myself no favors with school, I had the best time that afternoon. Just me and Grandad in the park, trying to control Trixie and laughing. Lots of laughing. Don't get me wrong. I missed school. I missed hanging out with Andrew. And there was a part of me that felt I maybe should have thought about my protest more clearly, perhaps taken other people's feelings more into account. Yes, there was some guilt there.

Funnily enough, I didn't even think about Destry Camberwick until we were back at Grandad's place. And when I did think about her, my pulse didn't exactly race. It jogged along at a healthy tick, true, but it didn't *race*.

37

ON THE DAY OF MILLTOWN'S GOT TALENT, THE DAY I
returned from suspension, I half expected to get a text message
from my mysterious sender. Maybe words of encouragement,
or even a question about whether I was doing it at all. There'd
been no communication since the last challenge was set, and
I didn't know whether this was confidence that I would rise
to the occasion or a loss of interest.

Andrew caught up with me at recess.

"I was talking to Destry Camberwick today and the conversation turned to you."

Now, I seem to remember saying something along the
lines that the mention of Destry's name no longer caused
my heart to race. Well, I might have been jumping the gun.
Andrew's words punched me in the gut, and my heart tried
to escape from my chest, desperate for freedom and batter-
ing at my ribs. I fought to gain control. It was important to

be cool about this news, maybe raise an eyebrow and say something along the lines of "Destry who?"

"OH, MY GOD!" I shrieked. "What did she say about me?"

"We were talking about your protest outside the cafeteria," said Andrew.

"Yes?"

"And she said she thought it was cool."

"What?"

"Cool. She said it was cool."

I was tempted to hit him, but obviously this was a situation that required all my tact and diplomacy.

"Andrew," I said. "Give me the whole conversation, right now, or I'm going to kick your head in."

Andrew looked puzzled. "I can't *remember* the whole conversation," he said. "Can I just give you the highlights?"

"'Cool' was a highlight?"

Andrew sighed. "Okay. I was talking about how bad the cafeteria is, how it serves the same food day after day. You know: 'Why can't we have a choice? Now the only options are fries, nachos, and hot dogs.' And she said, 'Yeah and burgers or corn dogs.' And I said . . ."

"Yes, all right, Andrew. Get to what was said about me, please. I don't need the whole conversation."

"But you just said you *did* need the whole conversation. You said—"

"Don't tell me what *I* said. Tell me what *she* said. I know what I said. I don't know what she said."

"I hate you sometimes, Rob. I think you should know that."

I waved an encouraging hand.

Andrew sighed again. "Okay. Destry said, 'Wasn't that your friend, Rob someone, who did the protest outside the cafeteria that day?'"

"She knew my name?"

"Only the first one. Unless you've changed your last name to Someone and forgot to tell me."

"She knows my first name," I whispered. A rosy glow swept through my entire body.

"And I said to her, 'Sure. Rob Fitzgerald, possibly the greatest, most committed, and kindest person in the state. Maybe Australia. Certainly in this school.'"

"You didn't say that!"

"No, I didn't. But I wished I had ten minutes later, when it was too late. Don't you hate it when that happens?"

"And then what did she say?"

"And then she said that was cool."

"That was it?"

"What else do you want?"

"She said *it* was cool or *I* was cool?"

"I dunno. God. I'm beginning to wish I hadn't mentioned it."

"Me too."

Andrew got up from the bench. I knew I'd annoyed him because his eyes were stony and his mouth a thin line. He was a dead ringer for Mum, apart from gender, age, and dress sense. "I tellya one thing," he snarled. "The only reason I mentioned all that stuff about the cafeteria was because I was trying to help you—you know, be a friend, a mate. I was fishing for some comment about you. Why would I complain about the cafeteria only doing burgers, fries, and nachos? I *only eat* burgers, fries, and nachos. I wish I hadn't bothered, Rob. You're an ungrateful dipstick."

I deflated then. "Sorry, Andrew," I said. "I didn't want to make you feel how sharper than a serpent's tooth it is to have a thankless friend."

He stuck a finger right between my eyes.

"Are you doing that Shakespeare thing again?"

"Sorry," I said. "*King Lear* this time."

"I hate it when you do that," he said. But I knew we were okay. I'm a good judge of tone.

38

"GRANDAD?" I SAID.

He grunted. We sat on a bench in front of the lake at the Old Farts' Palace. There was a central fountain, but something was wrong with it and it gave off a halfhearted dribble, like a tired garden hose. "Reminds me of my bladder," Grandad mumbled. He was in a grumpy mood despite having beaten me twice at chess. I could tell by the way he threw pieces of bread *at* the ducks rather than *for* them. They didn't appear to care. Mind you, Grandad the Grump wasn't exactly news.

"Thanks for sharing, Pop," I said. "I'm not sure I could've gone another day without an update on your bladder problems."

"Don't mention it, young Rob . . ."

"Tell me about Grandma," I said.

He stopped midthrow and gave me a fierce glare. Pop's

eyes are often bloodshot, and today was no exception, so he was only faintly scary. I smiled, but that made no difference. We sat for four, five beats, not breaking eye contact. I could see out of the corner of my eye a few ducks staring up at us, puzzled, presumably, by the sudden cease-fire. We were a frozen tableau. Apart from the fountain, which was still dribbling.

"Why?" said Grandad eventually. It was like he was squeezing the word out between reluctant lips.

"Because I don't know anything about her."

"So what's the problem?" Grandad finally returned his gaze to the lake. He broke off another chunk of bread and tossed it to a gaggle of ducks. They cringed instinctively as he raised his arm, and then got into a group fight over the morsel.

"I don't know anything about your life, Grandad," I said. "Not really. I know you were married, but I don't know who to. I have no idea whether she died or whether you divorced. Were you happy, were you miserable? What happened when it all ended . . . ?"

"Rob . . ." Pop raised a hand in the stop sign, but I wasn't in the mood to shut up. I'd spent most of my life shutting up when told to do so, and I was tired of it.

"You've kept secrets from me, Grandad, and I hate it." I felt my eyes welling up. This was stupid. Why was I crying? I hadn't felt emotional before. I hadn't intended to bring this subject up. All I'd thought about doing was what we normally do—hanging out together, being mates, cracking jokes. But now that I'd started, I couldn't stop. "You fought in a war, but you never talk about it. I don't even know which war it was. I asked Mum and she said you didn't like discussing it, so I thought to myself, 'Okay, I need to protect Grandad's feelings. He doesn't want to talk about something, so I should pretend it never happened. I should pretend my own grandmother never happened.'" There was plenty more I wanted to say, but tears were running down my cheeks and my throat was clamped off.

Grandad put one gnarled hand over mine, but I couldn't react. I couldn't even make eye contact.

"Rob, please," he said. "Please don't cry. I hate it when you cry. Listen, mate. Sometimes a person needs to keep things to himself. You don't tell me everything, and that's fine. We all need to keep some stuff locked away. If we didn't, then we could end up getting hurt. You know that. Even at your age, you know that."

"No," I said. "I'm not asking for *your* secrets. I'm asking for mine. I have a grandmother and she's a total stranger. I have a grandfather and I don't know much more about him. I'm your grandchild and you owe me answers. Otherwise . . ."

"Otherwise what?"

I sniffed and rubbed snot off my upper lip.

"Otherwise when you die, all I'll have is a cross stuck in the ground and question marks in my head."

There was a pause. Then Grandad laughed. But it was a gentle laugh.

"You've got me ahead of Agnes *and* Jim?" he said. "Wow. I didn't think I was looking *that* bad . . ."

"This is not a joke, Pop."

"No. You're right."

He stood and picked up his cane from where it was leaning at the side of the bench. He tried not to show it, but even the act of standing gave him pain. Just a brief flash in the eyes and then it was gone.

"Walk me back to my apartment, young Rob, and I'll tell you some things from my rather dull life," he said. "I lived through it once and, even for me, it seems unremarkable. But . . . not my problem if you want to be bored."

"Bore me, Grandad," I said. "Bore me stupid."

"You asked for it," he said. "And don't call me stupid."

I smiled.

"One other thing," he said. "No crosses."

"What?"

"I don't want a cross in the ground. Burn me please, Rob."

"Cremation?"

"That's it. Just make sure I'm dead first." Grandad headed up the winding path. Off to our right we could see Jim talking to the one duck not seduced by Grandad's artillery fire. "If I was you, I'd do it in a fire pit on the grounds here. It'd save a lot of money, but more importantly it'd annoy the blankety hell out of the mongrels who run this place."

"This isn't a subject for joking."

Grandad stopped. "Oh, young Rob," he said. "This is *exactly* a subject for joking. And anyway, I'm serious. Make a bonfire out of me in front of the fountain. Have a barbecue. That way I could annoy from beyond the grave while serving up a burger, and I can't tell you how happy that would make me. Except I'd be dead, of course. Still . . ."

"Grandad," I said. "Shut up."

He did.

Trust me, that doesn't happen often.

39

"I GO, AND IT IS DONE; THE BELL INVITES ME. HEAR IT not, Duncan; for it is a knell that summons thee to heaven or to hell."

I resisted the temptation to rush offstage, but it was difficult. The scene called for a quiet stalking—a half-determined, half-resigned Macbeth making his decision and walking, not only toward murder, but toward his own fate. Andrew told me later it looked like I'd pooed myself and was desperately trying to stop a large lump from dropping down my trouser leg onto the stage. He's not *always* supportive, Andrew.

When I got to the wings, I almost collapsed with exhaustion and nervous tension. But I kept to my trembling feet. This was the time, I knew, when applause from the audience—*the entire freaking school*—would tell me if I'd been successful or not, whether I'd connected with the audience. The previous act had been a heavy metal band and they'd gone down really well. The rafters hadn't exactly rung, but they'd kinda throbbed. A bit like the audience's heads. As I waited, I saw Destry Camberwick in my fevered imagination, eyes shining and brimming with tears, clutching her hands to her bosom and sighing as I left the stage.

Or maybe she was rolling on the floor in a fit of uncontrollable laughter.

There was silence after my act. This could be a good thing or a bad thing, I told myself. Possibly the audience was stunned by the power of my performance. It might take a few seconds for them to regain mastery of their emotions and then the applause would echo, not just ringing in the rafters but maybe bringing them down altogether.

Here's some context.

I'd spent an agonizing fifteen minutes backstage waiting my turn. All the symptoms of panic attacks battered at me. I had difficulty breathing, as if the atmosphere was solid. It was like trying to breathe in jagged rocks, and my airway could not get them down. There was a ringing in my ears (even before the heavy metal band) and I thought I was going to vomit. I tried all the tactics. I breathed deeply. I used some relaxation techniques that had helped in the past. It made no difference; I was still terrified. I waited while the other acts performed. All of them appeared to be having fun—confident and happy even when the acts themselves fell apart. There were three bands, a bad comedian, and someone who did impersonations that no one recognized. Even he got a decent round of applause.

Here's my result:

I died.

That's a show business term.

I died.

The students didn't even hate it. Boos would at least have been evidence of a connection. Storming the stage and running me out of town, tarred and feathered on a pole, would've been a *reaction*, if not the one I'd hoped for. Only the staff applauded and, I suspect, Andrew. How can you tell it's staff applauding and not students? No idea, but I'm certain it's true. Pity and professional duty rippled through the air toward me.

Looking back, I should've guessed the response. My act and a boring English class were twins separated at birth, and it probably wouldn't have surprised the audience if I had assigned them an essay when I was done. Maybe I'd put them straight to sleep like a stage hypnotist.

It didn't matter.

You see, I'd done it. I'd gone onstage and performed in front of eight hundred people. Who cared if they didn't like it?

Well, me, to be honest. But I'd survive.

I was beginning to think I could survive almost anything.

40

THE SCHOOL HAD MADE ME APOLOGIZE TO THE CAFETERIA
staff before I could take part in the talent show.

Milltown insists on a meeting between you, your parents, and the assistant principal for student welfare, before you can come back after suspension. Grandad wanted to be a part of that meeting but Mum and Dad had said no. I think if Grandad had showed up, staff would have dived under desks, texted final messages to loved ones, and called for police backup. As it was, Mum and Dad had nodded at everything the AP had said, glancing disapprovingly at me from time to time. I half expected they'd get on their knees and kiss his shoes, but that didn't happen.

The apology to the cafeteria staff was embarrassing.

"I'm sorry if I offended you," I'd said to Mrs. Appleby. I was going to add that it wasn't a protest directed at her personally, but I wanted to get the apology over with as quickly as possible.

"Didn't offend me, dear." Mrs. Appleby is a large and forbidding woman with an enormous bosom that seems like an impossible burden to lug around. When she turns in your direction, you feel you're in the line of fire. "I agree with you, actually," she continued. "The stuff we sell here is filth."

The AP tried to get the conversation back on track.

"The important point," he said, "is that Rob did the wrong thing—"

Mrs. Appleby ignored him. She didn't even move her bosom toward him, but the AP shut up anyway.

"Fried rubbish. Fries, fries, and more fries. God knows how many heart attacks we're storing up for the next generation . . ."

"Yes, thank you, Mrs. Appleby—"

"I've told them," she said. "But no one listens. 'How about salads?' I said. 'Oh, no. There's no profit in them. Give them cholesterol until it seeps out their pores.' Take children's money and give 'em poison in return. We're drug dealers, really, selling death, and caring only about money . . ."

"Well, thank you, Mrs. App—"

"A few burgers, made from stuff that should be thrown away—gut linings, brains, livers, and gonads . . ."

"Yes—"

"I won't eat it and I won't let my family eat it either," said Mrs. Appleby. "Not in a fit. For growing minds and bodies you need—"

"Mrs. Appleby." The AP was becoming agitated. "You *run* this cafeteria."

"Yes," she said, turning toward him. He flinched as her bosom caught him in its crosshairs, but he didn't duck. "For a franchise owner who doesn't care about healthy eating. But I've had enough. I'm out of here." She picked her handbag up from the counter.

"But you can't leave now, Mrs. Appleby," said the AP. "The first lunch break is about to start . . ."

It didn't matter. Mrs. Appleby charged toward the staff parking lot, scattering small children as she went. The AP and I watched in silence until she'd disappeared from view. Finally he turned toward me.

"I hope you've learned something from this, Rob," he said.

I nodded in what I hoped was a shamefaced fashion.

"Absolutely," I said.

(Mrs. Appleby, incidentally, returned five minutes after she'd stormed off.

"Bag of chips, love?" she asked as she went past.

"I thought you'd gone," I said.

"Only for a smoke," she replied. "I need to earn a living, and those deep fryers won't start themselves, you know.")

So I'd sat at my normal table at the front of the cafeteria, eating fries, thinking about my upcoming performance in Milltown's Got Talent and hoping the fries wouldn't make a dramatic reappearance onstage.

41

MONDAY. I SAT AT MY NORMAL TABLE IN FRONT OF THE
cafeteria, eating fries, and reliving my performance in
Milltown's Got Talent.

Daniel Smith paced off to my right, in front of the boys'
toilets. Miss Pritchett paced somewhere to my left. Daniel
often stakes a claim outside the toilets, presumably in the
hope I'll have to go and Miss P won't be able to follow. I
could tell him that I *never* go to public toilets. Ever. That
I would sooner die than use anything other than my own
bathroom in my own house. But I figured he didn't really
need that information, and anyway, if he wanted to hang
around the boys' room in a creepy fashion, who was I to
interfere?

Nonetheless, he obviously got bored because occasionally he'd take a step toward me, but Miss Pritchett would do
the same and he'd be forced to back off. Then he'd try again

when he thought she wasn't looking, and the whole thing would repeat.

It was like a slow and strange dance. Or a boring gif. They should've entered the talent show with it. It would've been more popular than my act.

I kept my head down and stuffed another fry into my mouth. A shadow fell across the seat opposite. I didn't need to look up. Only one person sits with me—two, if you count Daniel Smith, though he normally stands to inquire whether the cat's got my tongue. And he was still dancing with Miss P.

"Do you think I'm a blankety loser?" I asked. "Be honest."

"It's possible," said an angelic voice. "But you can't always trust first impressions."

My head shot up, just as my jaw plummeted and my eyes tried to leave their sockets. Sweat dripped off my forehead and made an impressive lake on the bench's surface. I attempted to speak, but my brain had shut down and buggered off to parts unknown.

Destry Camberwick sat down opposite me.

She was as gorgeous in real life as . . . well, I'd only ever seen her in real life, of course. But she'd never sat opposite me before. This was real. It was *really* real. There was nothing unrealistic about this real.

"Uh, uh, uh, um, um, uh," I said, obviously trying to *prove* I was a blankety loser. She put her hand out to me across the table. A portion of her hair fell across her left eye and she had to brush it back. A small part of me shriveled and died.

"I'm Destry," she said.

"I know," I said. Then I wanted to bite my tongue. Why had I said that? The obvious answer was, *Really? Pleased to meet you. I'm Rob Fitzgerald, but you can call me Rob or Fitz, if you like. Friends call me Fitz.* They didn't, of course, because I don't have friends, plural. I have a friend, singular, called Andrew, and he calls me Rob.

I took her hand and we shook. Another part of me shriveled and died.

"I'm Rob," I said.

"I know," said Destry. "I saw you in Milltown's Got Talent."

"I was the one proving the title wrong," I said. This was better. My brain had returned from its vacation, apparently refreshed. What was coming out of my mouth not only made sense, but was witty and self-deprecating. Maybe she'd realize I was not just a blankety loser, but a *witty* blankety loser. I'd settle for that.

"I thought you were great," she said.

Another small part shriveled and died inside. The way this conversation was going, I'd crumble into dust when I tried to stand.

"Thanks," I said.

"I love *Macbeth*," she said. "And I thought you did a fabulous job of showing his insecurity just before he goes off to murder Duncan." She liked Shakespeare! This was getting better and better. If I could just stop shriveling and dying . . . "You know, all anyone remembers is that Macbeth's a monster, but at the start of the play he's a decent guy."

She said a few more things, and in time I might remember what they were. But right then, all I noticed was the way the sun caught her face, the gleam of her hair, the small gap between her front teeth, and the hammering of my heart.

And then she was gone. A smile and a wave and back to her table on the far side of the cafeteria area.

I should've done better. I know that. Virtually the first words she heard me utter were swearwords, I'd made one fairly intelligent remark, and the rest was stumbling, bumbling, and bordering on gibberish. She, on the other hand, had been smart and interesting.

No. I'd blown it big-time.

But you couldn't wipe the smile off my face for the rest of the day.

42

OKAY. POETIC ATTEMPT NUMBER ONE HUNDRED AND five (not that I'm counting).

What about borrowing a line or two of well-known poetry, just to get me started? And rather than being afraid of rhyme, perhaps I should embrace it fully. It's worth a try, if only because everything else has been a disaster.

> *If I should die, think only this of me:*
> *Bury me, not in some random cemetery,*
> *But next to my true love, my Destry.*
> *(Assuming she's dead, of course.*
> *If not, that would be*
> *A total disaster, an undeniable tragedy.)*
> *I don't mean that if she was alive, it would be*
> *A bad thing. On the contrary . . .*

Excuse me while I stab myself in the hand with a sharp pencil.

Right. It's official. I just have to hope that Milltown's Got Talent impressed Destry enough, because I've given up on poetry.

Actually, I think it's given up on me.

43

"ARE YOU KIDDIN'?" SAID ANDREW. "THAT SOUNDS LIKE an awesome opportunity to me."

I'd finally told him about the chance of joining the state under-sixteen soccer squad and the possibility of going to Brisbane to play in a tournament. Mr. Broadbent was pushing for an answer, but with everything that had happened, I hadn't given it much thought. To be honest, I hadn't *wanted* to give it much thought. The enrollment forms were still in my bag, probably all crumpled and dog-eared by now.

"But I'd be away from home."

"Oh my God," said Andrew. He clutched the sides of his head in mock horror. "Not away from home! It's impossible. Can't be done. What on earth were they thinking?"

"All very well for you to make fun," I said, "but you don't suffer from panic attacks, Andrew."

"You get them at home, don't you?"

"You know I do."

"So how do you cope with panic attacks here?"

I thought about it. "Generally, I wait them out. Go someplace I can be alone, do my breathing exercises, and pass the time until the terror leaves." It always did. Eventually. "Strenuous exercise can help."

"So who do you talk to? Who holds you and calms you and tells you it'll all be okay?"

"No one."

"So if you get over it by yourself and no one else can help, what difference does it make where you are? And strenuous exercise helps, huh?" He leaned forward and knocked his knuckles against my head. "Duh. Soccer tournament. Hullo?"

"I'll get *more* panic attacks if I'm somewhere strange." I rubbed my head because that had *hurt*.

"Brisbane's not that strange. A bit, maybe . . ."

"You know what I mean."

"Hey, look," he said with a shrug. "If you're determined not to go, then I can't persuade you. I don't *want* to persuade you. But you asked my opinion and I gave it. 'Sup to you what happens next."

I hate it when Andrew is all logical. Because I knew what he said made sense. Panic attacks are personal and no one else *can* help. It's you, and you alone, facing the terror, dealing with a heart like an engine racing and screaming, threatening to shake you apart.

Yes. Panic attacks are lonely. But at least I can deal with them in a comfortable, familiar place.

Then again, why always take the comfortable and familiar path? Playing in that soccer game had been way outside my comfort zone, but I didn't regret doing it. And Mr. Broadbent seemed to think I was good enough. I took out my phone and went back to that first text message.

Do not fear fear. Its only purpose is to let you know that something is worth doing.

Maybe I *should* stop fearing fear.

"It's up to you, Rob," said Mum. "I mean, that's great they want you. But in the end it's a decision only you can make."

Dad pointed a sausage at me, which was slightly unnerving.

"I only wish someone had offered me a chance to play golf at state level," he said. "Imagine what my life might be like now. I could be on a golf course every day."

"You *are* on a golf course every day," Mum pointed out.

"Yeah, but the course would pay me to do it, instead of the other way round."

"Dad," I said. "I think you need to face facts."

He waved his sausage, which was still unnerving, but I interpreted it as encouragement to continue.

"You're rubbish at golf," I said. "And I should know because I watch you all the time."

"Rubbish? That's a little hurtful."

"The last round you played, you scored one hundred and twelve."

"That was a bad day."

"That was a *good* day."

He put the sausage back on his plate. I was relieved because it was looking absolutely wonderful and I'm vegetarian.

"But if I'd had encouragement, maybe I'd be better," he said. "Maybe I'd be a world-beater." A world-beater? I didn't think so. Possibly an eggbeater, but I didn't have the heart to say it out loud. So I turned back to Mum.

"What about my shyness?" I asked.

"What about it?"

"It'll be horrible in Brisbane because I won't know anyone and my shyness will mean I'll be all alone."

"Hey, look," she said with a shrug. "If you're determined not to go, then I can't persuade you. Because you'll always find an excuse, no matter what anyone says."

"Just do it," said Grandad. "If it doesn't work, then come home. Jeez, Rob. The younger generation always blankety overthinks things." He sucked on his teeth and treated me to a whistling rendition of some accidental tune that was actually quite nice.

"But I'd have to get changed in dressing rooms and use public toilets, Pop. You know I don't have the confidence to do that sort of stuff."

"Then get over yourself, young Rob. You *know* what I think, because we've talked about this before. Accept who you are and stop worrying how others are going to react."

"Easy for you to say."

"Hey, look," he said with a shrug. "If you're determined not to go, then I can't persuade you. But all I will say is: don't end up with regrets. You will, of course. Everyone does. But don't rack 'em up unless you have to."

He paused. "Fancy a game of chess?" he said. "You won't regret it."

I got the next text message that same night. At ten thirty-five.

**Here's a challenge that will challenge.
Accept it or decline. "Carpe diem" or
"dedo." Look it up, my friend.**

**Get yourself onto the front page of the
local newspaper.**

It doesn't matter how you do it.

I already knew that "carpe diem" meant "seize the day." But I had to look up "*dedo*" on my phone. It's Latin for "surrender."

44

"I FIRST SAW YOUR GRANDMOTHER IN SYDNEY IN 1962. I was twenty-three years old and literally fell over her in Darling Harbour."

Grandad had his cane between his legs and he'd propped his chin against the handle. I sat next to him on the couch in his apartment and we stared out through the window toward the distant lake. A few ducks wandered around, and the fountain gurgled and belched, though we couldn't hear it. Grandad occasionally gurgled and belched as if to provide the missing sound effects.

"You have to understand," he said, "that Darling Harbour was very different in those days. It was probably a good twenty years before Neville Wran made it into the upmarket place it is now. Then, it was an industrial area gone to seed, a place that had outlived its usefulness."

"You bumped into Gran," I reminded him. This was not

the time for social history. I was about to learn something about my grandmother, and I was excited.

"She was carrying a bag of groceries, and it spilled all over the street." He laughed as he watched it in his mind. "She said afterward it was my fault, that I'd been running along the street and hadn't paid attention. Just barged straight into her, sent the groceries flying. But it wasn't like that, Rob. I wasn't running. I walked. And *she* bumped into *me*. But she'd never admit that." His eyes took on a faraway look. "Your grandmother didn't brook arguments. She knew she was right, even when she was wrong."

"What was her name?" I asked. I needed basic information before we got into who was at fault about flying groceries more than fifty years ago. It didn't matter, at least to me. Maybe it did to Pop.

"Bella," said Grandad. "'Beautiful' in Italian. And my God she deserved that name."

Bella. I knew my grandmother's name! I nearly burst into tears there and then. I'm such a crybaby. But I kept control because if I sobbed, Grandad would pay attention to me, and I wanted him to pay attention to his memories. To keep control I had to curl up my hands so my nails bit into my palms.

"I stood there dazed," said Grandad. "I couldn't believe how beautiful she was. It was like being hit over the head with something soft and heavy." He fell silent.

"Love at first sight," I offered.

"Maybe," said Pop. "Maybe that was it."

"What did she say?" I asked. I leaned forward on the couch, eager to catch every word. Pop's voice had softened and his eyes had become dreamy. I leaned a little more. I had only a portion of one butt cheek on the couch and worried I'd collapse into a heap on the floor unless Pop said something.

"She didn't," said Grandad. "She just looked at me with those brown eyes."

"And?" I said.

"And then she kneed me in the nuts," said Grandad.

This was so unexpected, I *did* slip off the couch and bruise my tailbone. It really hurt.

"She did not," I wailed.

"No, she didn't," agreed Grandad. "I made that up."

"I hate you, Grandad," I said.

"No, you don't," he said. "It's not my fault you're a romantic idiot, Rob."

"It's not my fault either," I pointed out. "So, was any of that true? Her name, your first meeting?"

Grandad stood and arched his back as if ironing out aches and pains.

"The violence was my only fiction," he said. "Your grandma's name was Bella and I met her by falling over her in 1962 in Darling Harbour. And she was beautiful. She was *so* beautiful."

"So what happened then?" Grandad was right. I *am* a

romantic idiot and this was a story that already had me on the edge of messy, hysterical sobbing.

"Ah," said Pop. "I didn't see her again for five years. But I never forgot her, Rob. Hardly a day passed in those intervening years when I didn't think about those eyes. I knew we were destined to meet again."

"Oh God, Grandad," I said. "That is *so* romantic." I couldn't help myself this time. It was like a wall had given way, and I burst into tears. Grandad put a hand on my shoulder.

"Without a doubt, Rob," he said, "you are the most spineless crybaby in the entire Southern Hemisphere."

"I know, Pop," I spluttered between sobs. "Maybe the world."

He didn't argue.

45

GET YOURSELF ONTO THE FRONT PAGE OF THE LOCAL newspaper.

It was obvious I was going to have problems with this task. A time for mature reflection on these texts and where they were leading me was obviously called for. I closed my eyes and concentrated.

First things first. Back to the thorny problem of who was sending them. I had a short list of two—Mum and Dad (one person) and Grandad. I'd never heard any of them use Latin, but I supposed that wasn't a clinching argument, on the grounds that I'd never heard *anyone* use Latin. *Get yourself onto the front page of the local newspaper.* That's not something a parent would suggest, especially since it also said *It doesn't matter how you do it.* Maybe if it had said *Get yourself onto the front page of the newspaper for charitable services to the community,* then I'd keep Mum and Dad as suspects. But the text encouraged me to do *anything* to get there. Holding up the local McDonald's with a sawn-off shotgun, tying myself naked to a statue in the Central Business District, stealing a car and ramming it into a storefront. There were plenty of possibilities, but Mum and Dad certainly wouldn't be encouraging them. They'd gone ballistic when I'd stood in front of the cafeteria with a sign, for God's sake. I couldn't see them being character witnesses at my trial for urban terrorism, arguing that at least I'd made it onto the front page of the local newspaper and all should therefore be forgiven.

It *couldn't* be them.

Unless they trusted my judgment on what would be acceptable and unacceptable actions to achieve the challenge.

No. It *really couldn't* be them.

That left Grandad. What did Sherlock Holmes say? When you've eliminated the impossible, whatever remains, however improbable, must be the truth.

Grandad.

What was becoming increasingly obvious was that these challenges were designed to improve my self-confidence. I'd spent most of my life trying to be as small as possible, scuttling through the world unobserved. The sender of the texts was trying to widen my experience, putting me center stage and proving I had no reason to be self-conscious. And, I had to admit, it was working. Thus it followed that the sender was someone who cared about me. Cared *for* me.

As far as I knew, only four people did that, and I'd eliminated three. You can't argue with Sherlock.

Grandad.

I was dimly aware of muffled laughter. I opened my eyes and nearly wet myself.

Ms. Singh's face was inches from mine. Now, her face is lovely—it's just that I wasn't expecting it to fill my vision. So I jumped a surprising and possibly impossible distance off my chair.

"Sorry to disturb you, Rob," she said. The laughter increased. "It's just that I've asked you three times for the solution to this problem. After the first, I figured you were sleeping. After the third I was afraid you were dead. Believe me, I'm happy to know you're still in the land of the living."

"Sorry, Miss," I said. "I was thinking."

"Excellent. That makes a welcome change. So you have the solution?"

"Er, I wasn't actually thinking about *math*. Sorry, Miss."

"No apologies necessary, Rob. We can work on the problem together during lunchtime detention today. How does that sound?"

Blankety awful was the reply, but I kept that in my head.

"Okay," I mumbled.

"No, no, no, Rob. Definitely not 'okay.' My lunch is my lunch, and the last thing I want is to spend it with students, particularly a student who wasn't paying attention during the time I *am* paid to teach. 'Okay,' I'm afraid, doesn't cut it."

I thought for a moment.

"Thank you, Ms. Singh."

"You're welcome, Rob," she said.

We didn't work on the problem. *I* worked on it, while Ms. Singh ate a small salad and marked assignments. At least it gave me an opportunity to get out my phone, though I kept it hidden beneath the desk.

Do you really mean ANYTHING, Grandad? I texted back.

I wasn't expecting a reply. True, I'd got one once, but that was only in response to a yes-or-no question. The other times I'd texted, I'd gotten zilch.

Nonetheless, my phone buzzed.

Whatever it takes, said the text message. **And this isn't your grandfather.**

"Checking your phone during detention?" said Ms. Singh. How could she sneak up on me like that? Was she a ninja? "I think that means another meeting tomorrow lunchtime, Rob. What do you think?"

I thought.

"Thanks, Ms. Singh," I said. "It's quality time, and I really enjoy it."

46

"MUM?" I SAID.

I tried to keep the tone conversational, quiet, and reasonable. Just a normal question on a normal day.

"What?" Mum wrapped the roast in aluminum foil and placed it in the oven. It was beef. It was disgusting. Not only had an innocent animal died to fill that piece of foil, but the cost to the environment was enormous. It was clear that putting the meat into the oven was a betrayal of the planet and a damning verdict on humanity.

It was also clear I'd need to stay away from the kitchen when the smells started coming from the oven. I can resist everything except temptation . . .

"Can I have a dog?" I peeled a carrot in what I hoped was a casual fashion. "Please?" I added, because manners never hurt.

"I'm sorry?"

"Apology accepted."

"No. What did you say?"

"A dog." I decided to keep my sentences short in the hope that the fewer the words, the foggier the meaning. Plus, I mumbled. Maybe Mum would say yes if she thought I was asking for a log. *You want a log, Rob? Go for it.* Or a cog. Or a bog. Or a hog. Okay, maybe not a hog.

"Are you insane?" said Mum.

"Is that a trick question?" I replied.

"Did you just ask for a dog?"

"Maybe."

"You *are* insane!"

I put the peeled carrot into a pan and picked up another. To be honest, I was very careful in my handling. Mum's comments about vegetables had scared me a little. What if they *did* feel pain? What if this carrot was silently screaming, *Please don't strip off my skin with a sharp blade clearly designed for the purpose of torturing, not just me, but my friend the potato and other sundry tubers? What sick mind could design that implement?* I gritted my teeth and continued peeling. Mum could trim them. That was, for me, a step too far.

"It's not *really* a dog," I said.

"That's a relief," said Dad. He was in charge of the gravy. "I thought you asked if you could have a dog. You know, a canine."

"That's what I thought," said Mum.

We all chuckled at the misunderstanding.

"I apologize," I said. "What I should have said was, Can I please have a fluffy bundle of rubbish?"

Agnes asked if she could come with me on my after-school walk with Trixie, and I was happy to agree. It was basically her dog, after all, and it's not like I was a stranger to walking around town with an old person in tow.

If I'd ever cared about street credibility (which I hadn't), it'd been destroyed a long time ago.

"You'll have to stop regularly and let me catch my breath," she said. "I'm not as young as I used to be."

I scratched my head. "Neither am I," I said. "Do you know anyone who is?"

"You're like your grandfather," she said.

"Thank you."

"It wasn't meant as a compliment."

"Okay," I said. "Fair point."

We walked for an hour, but that included multiple stops while Agnes caught her breath. In a sense, we were lucky. It was that time of the afternoon between school finishing and people coming home from work, so there weren't many dog walkers on the streets. This pleased Trixie, who, and I think I might have mentioned this before, took the presence of another dog as a personal insult.

Trixie was at least an equal-opportunity bully. In the

absence of dogs, she went for people. Anyone who came within snarling distance.

"What's her problem?" I asked Agnes.

"She's a fluffy bundle of rubbish," Agnes replied. "To her, all the rest of the world is a problem." She stopped and fanned herself, even though it wasn't very hot. "You know," she added, "I find that dog both annoying and adorable in turn."

I opened my mouth, but Agnes held up a hand.

"Annoying, because . . . well." She sighed. "She finds *everything* irritating. I'm old, Rob, and I take pride in being irritable. I've earned the right over many years, and no one is going to take it away from me. Everyone should have a hobby. But I can't keep up *constant* irritation. It's too exhausting."

"And adorable?" I prompted.

"Adorable, because she sees no limit on her power and ability. Look at her." I did. The dog was in one of her more frenzied states, possibly because a very large man was crossing the road a hundred yards ahead of us. He might have been a sumo wrestler and was therefore fair game for a terrier that wouldn't tip ten pounds on the scales. *C'mon, coward*, she seemed to be snarling. *Give it your best shot, punk. I can take you.*

"She's delusional," I said.

Agnes started walking again.

"Or a suffragette," she said.

"I beg your pardon?"

"A suffragette," said Agnes. "You know what a suffragette is?"

"Yes. We did a politics unit last semester. A suffragette was a woman who campaigned for equal rights, particularly getting the vote, at a time when women were thought to be second-class citizens."

Agnes was breathing pretty hard. She put a hand across her chest.

"Do you mind if we sit on that bench for a while, Rob?"

It took a couple of minutes before she could speak again.

"Yes. That's what a suffragette was. And some would say women are *still* considered second-class citizens. But you don't understand the odds a suffragette faced back then. She had no power, no influence. No one cared what she thought, because the world was run by men. Still is, unfortunately. So no one was on her side, except some other women. Not all, I'm sad to say, but some. Yet, despite those massive handicaps, they changed the world."

I kept silent. This was interesting and, anyway, I got the impression Agnes was talking more to herself than anything else.

"That's why I love this dog. She doesn't care that she has no power. She's not the slightest bit bothered that the odds are stacked against her. She howls and gnashes against the status quo, and who's to say she won't be successful in the long term?"

"So Trixie's a feminist?" I said.

"Exactly," said Agnes. "And feminists are the world's best people."

"Trixie's a dog," I pointed out.

"You're like your grandfather," said Agnes.

"No need to insult me," I said.

"He's not all bad," said Agnes. "Where's your respect?"

I kept quiet. Sometimes it's important to cut your losses when there's no chance of winning an argument.

"A fluffy bundle of rubbish?" said Mum.

"Or a feminist," I said. "Possibly a suffragette. Depends which definition you prefer."

47

"WHAT HAPPENED THEN?"

Grandad got up from the couch and straightened a picture on the wall. He cocked his head to check the angle, then sat down again. Even that small movement left him slightly breathless.

"What? After I saw your grandmother for the first time?"

"Yes. Pop! You know what I'm talking about."

"Well, I picked up her groceries and helped her repack them. Then I believe I tipped my hat to her and wished her a good morning. She thanked me. At least I think she thanked me, but it was half a century ago so my memory could be playing tricks."

Grandad got up again and opened a door in the cabinet that housed his television. I couldn't remember the last time I'd seen the TV on, but he must watch it *sometimes*. Grandad knows more about what's going on in the world than anyone else I know. He reached into the cabinet and pulled out the chess set. "Fancy a game, Rob?" he said.

"Only if you let me win," I said. We'd now played many times and I'd never won a game. Not once. Not even close. This isn't really surprising because I'm thirteen; Pop is older than God's dog and therefore has a massive advantage. When he was growing up, he probably only had chess to play. My generation has computers. I should challenge him to a first-person shooter game on my console. Then again, knowing Grandad's competitive streak, he'd probably beat me.

"You're kidding, right?" said Grandad.

"No."

"You need to understand one thing," said Pop, returning to the couch and setting up the board. "I will never, *ever* let you beat me at chess. You could be dying of leukemia, as bald as your father, with an hour left to live, and I wouldn't let you win. I'd crush you. And then I'd taunt you about it while you took your dying breath."

"Fine words, Pop," I said. "You're making me tear up."

"You wouldn't *want* me to let you win," said Pop.

"Yes, I would," I said. "I just told you that."

"And what would such a victory be worth? Tell me that, young Rob."

"It would mean I'd beaten you for once." I placed my white queen on the white space at the back of the board. "That's important to me now. If I was about to take my last breath, it would mean even more."

"No," said Grandad.

"Yes," I said.

The board was set up and I moved my king's pawn a couple of spaces forward. Grandad mirrored my move.

"You remember your soccer game?" he said.

"Sure."

"What if I told you every member of that opposition team deliberately didn't try? That I had been in touch with them before the game and offered them fifty bucks each *not* to try."

"You didn't, did you?" You could never tell with Grandad. He waved a hand.

"Of course not. But answer my question."

I didn't want to because I knew where the conversation was going. Achievements aren't worthy of the name unless they're a genuine result of talent and commitment. Undeserved victory would taste like ashes in the mouth. I knew all this, even as I moved a knight forward and took another step toward inevitable defeat.

"No," I said. "Answer *my* question. When did you see my grandmother next?"

Grandad saw Bella again in late 1967. He was walking through Darling Harbour with a couple of mates—the first time he'd been back in those intervening years, he said—when he saw a woman on the other side of the street. Maybe it was because she wasn't moving and everything else was, but his eyes were drawn to her.

Or maybe it was destiny.

He stopped. His mates kept going. Pop gazed at Bella, and the world went about its business without either of them. For a while, neither moved. Then he walked over; she stayed still. Even when he stood a matter of inches from her, she didn't react.

"Hello," he said.

She didn't smile. She shifted her weight onto her right hip and cocked her head to one side. Grandad *thought* she cocked her head, but he couldn't be one hundred percent certain. But he remembered her next words exactly.

"I've waited five years," she said. "Where have you *been*, you mongrel?"

"Checkmate," said Pop.

"Congratulations," I said. "You've crushed a thirteen-year-old and I hope you're proud of yourself."

"I am," he said. "I beat you in twenty-five moves, which I think is my best result against you."

"If I was taking my last breath, your victory would be even sweeter," I said.

"Oh, Rob," said Grandad. "Don't be childish."

"I *am* a child," I said.

"Doesn't mean you have to behave like one."

"Okay," I said. I set up the pieces for a new game. I didn't really care about losing because I was, despite Pop's words, getting better. I was beginning to see the patterns, and how a move might have ripples across time.

Like Pop and Bella meeting in a street in Sydney in 1967.

"Tell me your answer," I continued.

"To what?"

"To Grandma's question. Where *had* you been in those five years, you mongrel?"

48

I'M NOT SURE WHY PEOPLE BOTHER TO COOK. I MEAN,
I know why cooking is necessary. Without it, we'd all starve to death, and I don't think I'm being too controversial when I say that would be a shame.

But it's so hard!

I watched a couple of daytime cooking shows on the television. There it seems easy. Celebrity chefs laugh, make interesting asides, all the while adding a pinch of this, a teaspoon of that, and a smidgeon of the other. No mess. Paintwork glistens, kitchen surfaces gleam, and then, suddenly, a magnificent dish appears as guests drool, studio audiences cheer, and credits roll.

No food preparation (those diced onions appear as if by magic).

No washing up.

Trust me: the real world is *very* different.

I mention this because I got into an argument with Dad that went something along the lines of:

Him: Vegetarian food is rubbish.

Me: No, it's not.

Him: Tofu and quinoa salad. That's not for human consumption. It's rabbit food and I wouldn't even wish it on a rabbit. Even if that rabbit was my worst enemy.

Me: Dad, you're talking rubbish. You don't know any rabbits, friendly or otherwise.

Him: But if I did, if I knew the worst rabbit in the world, the evil genius of the rabbit kingdom, the master rabbit terrorist, I wouldn't wish tofu and quinoa salad on it.

Me: I can't believe the garbage you're talking.

Him: I know. I'm having difficulty believing it myself. But answer me this: If humanity was meant to eat lettuce, why weren't we given teeth like tombstones and long, floppy ears?

Me: Dad, I'm thirteen and you're . . . old. Can we both start acting our ages? Vegetarian food is tasty, delicious, and good for the planet. Anyway, your ears are a bit floppy.

Him: Eating meat is part of human nature. Vegetarian food might be good for the planet. I'll give you that. But it is disgusting and that's why you don't have vegetarian drive-throughs. Can I supersize your lettuce? Would you like butter beans with that? Get real, Rob.

Me: I'll prove you wrong, Dad. I'll cook you a delicious vegetarian meal tonight, something so amazing, you'll probably give up steak forever.

Him: You're on. Tell you something, Rob. With a claim like that, the steaks couldn't be higher! Geddit? Steaks? Stakes?

Me: That's it. You're banned from computer games for the rest of the day.

Mum gave me money to get the ingredients from the supermarket, but she didn't offer me a lift there. She muttered something about learning what it's like to run a small part of the household without any help. Or thanks. I believe she was in something of a grumpy mood, so I avoided arguing.

Instead I looked up a recipe on the Internet, jotted down the ingredients, walked ten minutes to the supermarket, and spent thirty minutes tracking down the stuff I needed. (If you don't know your way around a supermarket, it can be a scary business. There are probably people who went in there for a cabbage and never emerged again. It wouldn't have surprised me to find a human skeleton in among the frozen peas.) Then I walked fifteen minutes home (the bags were heavy and slowed me considerably), unpacked, and spread out the ingredients on the kitchen counter.

To be honest I was exhausted already, but now was not the time to give up. I mean, how hard could it be? Just follow the recipe. It couldn't be rocket surgery. Or even brain science. I had this under control.

Did you know that if you don't spread a thin layer of

salt over sliced eggplant, the vegetable will taste bitter? The salt draws out moisture, so you have to keep it draining on kitchen towels. Unfortunately, we were out, so I used toilet paper. Not a good choice. The paper basically dissolved. Have you ever spent an hour picking small pieces of toilet paper off sliced eggplant? Of course you haven't. You'd have to be an idiot.

I wish to draw a veil over the next three hours. At one point Mum came into the kitchen and asked if it was my mission to use every single pot and pan in the household. I would've gotten angry at her sarcasm, but looking around, it was obvious I had used every single pot and pan in the household. It hadn't exactly been my *mission*, though.

At seven o'clock I put a casserole on the dining table and called Mum and Dad. They sat and examined the dish. Dad prodded it with a spoon.

"Is that toilet paper?" he asked.

"No," I lied. "It's vegetarian lasagna."

"It looks like charred toilet paper on the top."

"C'mon, Dad," I said. "That's a secret ingredient. And anyway, who in their right mind could identify toilet paper, charred or otherwise, in a casserole? You'd have to be some kind of sick person."

I spooned out a good helping for each of us. Breaking the crust of the lasagna was something of a challenge, and when I did, it produced a strange smell, which I tried to ignore.

"Enjoy," I said.

We each took a small bite. Three spoons clinked against three bowls. Dad stood and reached for his car keys.

"A veggie burger with large fries for me," I said. "Maybe an apple pie for dessert."

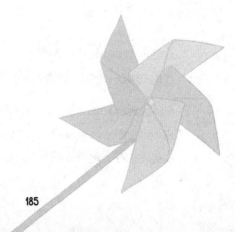

49

I THINK I MIGHT HAVE MENTIONED THAT I RARELY WATCH
television news. There's seldom any *good* news, and if I want
to depress myself, I'll just read a math textbook instead.

But sometimes it's on and sometimes a word or two reels
me in.

This time the words were "local slaughterhouse" and
"cruelty." I put my book down (*not* math) and paid attention, but the story was finishing and I didn't get all the
information. So I pulled out my phone and searched. Didn't
take long.

Local slaughterhouse's management professes ignorance of cruel practices filmed by employee

Shocking footage has emerged of animals being
ill-treated as they are led to slaughter in a local
slaughterhouse. A YouTube video of the cruelty has been

posted and shows sheep being brutally stabbed with an electric stunning device, while others are killed without being stunned properly, in contravention of regulations governing humane treatment of animals in Australia's processing plants. A management representative said the footage was posted by a disgruntled employee with an axe to grind. He said the company trained its workers in the correct procedures and that the disturbing images demonstrated that "rogue" workers were operating within the establishment. "We will root out these bad apples," he said. "We take the humane care of our animals very seriously."

I didn't want to, but I found the video on YouTube and forced myself to watch it. Then I went to the toilet and threw up. Afterward I did some more research.

I need your help, Andrew, I texted.

Wot 4

Want to be on the front page of the local newspaper for chaining yourself to a supermarket's railings to protest animal cruelty?

Sure y not

You say that like I've asked you to go
skateboarding. Don't you have any
questions?

No k maybe when

What?

When

Saturday.

Sure

You could be arrested and thrown in jail.
Gloom, destruction, end of life as we
know it. Criminal history. Massive parental
disappointment. Just for starters.

Cool

Why "cool"?

Satday free not doin anything else

You're an idiot.

Takes 1 to no 1

That's "know," idiot.

I no

I hate you.

I no

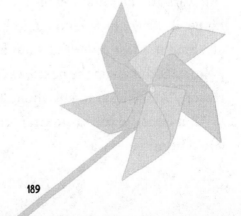

50

"I WENT AWAY TO WAR," SAID GRANDAD. "AND THEN, when I got back . . ."

"Whoa," I said. "Hold on to those horses, Pop. Which war?"

"It doesn't matter."

"Yes, it does."

"Oh, no. No, Rob. Trust me, it doesn't." Grandad was fierce, even by his own standards. He pointed his bishop at me like a loaded gun before returning it to the board. "All wars are the same. People kill each other. Then they go home, if they're lucky enough to be alive, and try to forget all about it. Most times that's impossible. In the meantime, politicians dream up the next war. And that's only one of the reasons I don't want to talk about it."

"But what did you say to Grandma when she asked where you'd been?" Pop was agitated but I couldn't let this go.

"I just told you. I'd been away to war."

"Didn't she ask you about it?"

"Yes. And I told her I didn't want to discuss it. She understood. People understood then. They don't now. You should be ashamed of yourself, Rob, if you take a moment to think about it."

"But . . ."

"Do you want to know about your grandmother, or not?"

I gazed at the chessboard. Even to my inexperienced eyes, it was clear I was in a hopeless position. A bit like the conversation I was having.

"I do, Grandad," I said.

She'd been waiting five years. Grandad, it seems, accepted this as a simple statement of fact. My first reaction would have been, *Why?* But, as Pop pointed out to me, I have a well-developed sense of my own worthlessness. It seems, in 1967, Grandad didn't suffer from the same problem. He was, on the surface at least, confident.

"What did you look like back in 1967, Grandad?" I asked.

"You don't want to know," he replied.

"Well, I do," I said, "or I wouldn't have asked."

"My hair," said Pop, "reached down to below my shoulders. It was all layered and shiny. And I had a spectacular handlebar moustache."

"A what?"

"A moustache that bent around the sides of my mouth

and came down to my chin. Huge sideburns . . ." He saw my puzzled expression and demonstrated at the side of his face. "Way past my ears and nearly reaching the ends of the moustache."

"Was there any part of you that wasn't hairy?" I said. It was difficult to get my head around the fact that my grandfather was more wombat than human. Now he was mostly shiny skin and deep lines.

"Not really," he replied. "You should've seen me in my bathing suit. I was ninety percent shag rug."

"Way too much information," I said.

"Told you, but you wouldn't listen. I have photographs somewhere. Unless you behave yourself, I'll get them out. And I haven't even got around to the fashion of the time. Paisley shirts. Flared trousers. You've been warned, young Rob."

This was *really* exciting. Grandad as a young man. I wasn't going to let that go, but I also sensed that if I asked him to get out the old albums now, I'd never hear more about Grandma.

"So Grandma told you she'd been waiting five years," I said. "What happened then?"

"I took her hand and said the wait had been worth it."

"You were a smooth talker, Pop."

"Check," said Grandad. Where did that come from? I gazed at the board. The position I was in was hopeless, but I couldn't resign. We'd been here before. According to Grandad I had to fight to the bitter end. Never give up.

Australians never give up, he'd said. *It's what makes us great as a nation.* I moved my king to a safe square.

"And then?" I said.

"And then I wooed her," said Grandad. "I wouldn't let her forget me. Not that she would have. I think I knew that even then." His voice had taken on a distant quality, as if he'd traveled back in time and was living those moments once more. "She was so beautiful, Rob. The most beautiful woman I'd ever known. We married in 1969. Your father was born in 1972."

"And then what happened?"

"To your father?"

"No." I hated it when Grandad deliberately messed with my head. "To Grandma."

"Ah," said Grandad. He thought for a moment and then moved a bishop the length of the board. "Checkmate," he said.

I examined the position. I don't know why. It was obviously checkmate. I sighed and set up the board again.

"She left me in 1975," Grandad said. "Went back to Italy. Was going to take your dad with her, but changed her mind at the last moment."

That news would take some processing. One decision taken or not taken more than forty years ago determined whether I was born or not. I'd always known, intellectually, that life was a matter of chance, but I'd never *felt* it until now.

"Why?" I whispered.

"I think she knew that if she'd taken your dad, I couldn't survive. She loved me enough to save my life by giving up her son to me." He rubbed at the stubble peppering his chin. "I heard she died in 2001."

He moved a pawn a couple of places forward on the board. I followed suit, though I couldn't concentrate. But when it came to digging out truths from Grandad's past, I knew I had to plan my moves far ahead. And be patient. One fact at a time.

"But why did she leave you?" I said. My grandmother was dead. I didn't really know how to feel. On the one hand, I hadn't known her, so it wasn't really a loss, as such. But a part of me shriveled to know that she'd *never* be more than a name to me.

It was sad. It was very sad.

"She couldn't deal with the ghosts," said Grandad.

"I beg your pardon?"

"She tried, but it was no good." Grandad rubbed at his mouth and moved his bishop, threatening my knight. "I came with ghosts, and although she gave it eight years of constant effort, she couldn't really compete. In the end, she had to leave. I was glad she did, because it was no life for her."

"Ghosts?" I moved my knight.

"I came back to Sydney in 1967 with a whole company of ghosts." Grandad sighed. "They were with me constantly then." He looked over to the corner of the room. "And to be honest, they're still with me, Rob. They've never really gone away."

I felt a chill, even though the evening was warm.

"Those ghosts," he continued. "I can't tell you how tempting it was back then to join them. But I had your dad to look after. To raise. It was your father who gave me a reason for living."

Grandad moved his rook.

"Check," he said.

51

IF I'M HONEST, IT'S NOT DIFFICULT TO GET ONTO THE FRONT page of the local newspaper. A couple of weeks back someone managed it by claiming they'd found a potato that looked like the prime minister. The newspaper sent not just a reporter but a photographer, too, who took shots of the spud from different angles. Now, I admit, a couple of blemishes on the potato's skin did give the impression of eyes (if you were *very* imaginative), but other than that it looked . . . like a potato.

The editor even put a photo of the PM next to the spud so readers could see for themselves. But it was never going to happen that someone would gaze at the pictures, scratching their head while muttering, *One of these is the leader of our nation and the other is the raw material for a packet of salt and vinegar chips, but I have no idea which is which.*

Anyway, this story not only dominated the front page but spilled onto page two as well, where a reporter debated which of the two was better suited to run the country (the potato narrowly lost on economic vision but won overwhelmingly on popular appeal).

The point I'm making is that the newspaper isn't known for investigative journalism. It's more school festivals, gardening tips, and cats stuck up trees. It shouldn't, therefore, have been difficult to interest it in a local story, particularly one with huge moral implications. Turns out it was. Maybe I should have claimed I owned a carrot that could communicate with extraterrestrials. That would have turned into a three-page spread.

"Good afternoon," I said.

Andrew and I had popped into the newspaper's offices after school on Friday. If I'd been expecting a large, noisy office with dozens of reporters all on phones, with the occasional cry of "Hold the front page" ringing out, then I would have been disappointed. A young man with acne sat behind a desk, staring at a computer screen. In the dim reflection of a picture hanging on the wall behind him I could see the game he was playing. He didn't reply, but after a minute or so, paused the game with an irritated clicking of his tongue (and his mouse).

"Can I help you?" he asked in a tone suggesting it was unlikely.

"We'd like to speak to a reporter," I said.

"That's me."

"Are you sure?" asked Andrew.

The guy looked around the bare office in an exaggerated way, as if in search of hiding colleagues. "Maybe there's someone else here but he's really good at camouflage," he said. "However, if you can't spot him in the next couple of minutes, we'll have to settle for me."

"Are the others out chasing leads?" I said. It's best to ignore sarcasm, in my humble opinion.

"The *other* is out having an ingrown toenail removed," he said. "Now, I'm very busy here, so what can I do for you?"

"I want to give you notice of a breaking story," I replied. "Tomorrow, at nine in the morning, the two of us will be chained to railings outside the shopping center on Mitchell Street, protesting the sale of meat by both the supermarket and the local butcher. That meat is sourced from the scandal-plagued slaughterhouse that's been dominating the news in recent days." I was pleased with myself. I thought I'd summarized the story well.

"You're chaining yourself to railings?" said the man. "I'm sorry. Why?"

I sighed. Maybe my summary hadn't been so good. Or maybe he simply hadn't been listening. I explained again.

"What scandal-plagued slaughterhouse?"

I reminded him about the video of the animals' illtreatment. He'd never heard of it. I had to get the story up on my phone. I even had to find the video so he could watch it. It was disturbing to discover that our local newspaper was ignorant of important local news stories. Or maybe they only bothered with breaking potato newsflashes and left everything else to other agencies.

"And what's this to do with the shopping center?"

This time Andrew sighed. We were splitting up the sighing duties, even though we hadn't planned this beforehand.

"Because they get their meat from this slaughterhouse. It's tainted meat and that's what we're protesting about."

"By chaining yourself to railings?"

"Jeez," said Andrew. He has a short temper, if truth be told. "I'm not presenting you with a riddle puzzling the greatest scientific minds around the world. Yes. Chains. Padlocks. Protesting the supermarket and butcher selling meat that has been obtained through appalling cruelty."

"Does it have to be nine?" the man asked.

"I beg your pardon?"

"You said nine in the morning. Can you chain yourselves up a bit later?"

"Why?"

"I like to sleep in on Saturdays," he said. "How about midday?"

"Will you bring a photographer?"

"I *am* the photographer. Well, if I remember to bring my cell phone, which I'm pretty sure I will."

"Do you postpone *all* news stories so they don't clash with your sleep?" said Andrew.

"What?"

"You know. Calling the tsunamis to see if they wouldn't mind waiting a couple of hours, that kind of thing?"

"Hey, listen, you . . ."

"Okay," I said. A battle of sarcasm was only going to end badly. "Midday it is. Don't forget, now."

"Good point," the reporter said. "I'll put an alarm on my phone."

I wasn't convinced. When Andrew and I left the office, the man was playing his game again and swearing at the screen.

52

TRIXIE WAS GETTING USED TO ME AND I WAS GETTING
used to her. Agnes turned down the offer of a walk when I
got to the old-age home, citing breathlessness and a visit from
her daughter due that afternoon. I had a cunning plan, so
that was fine by me.

Well, it wasn't really a plan and it certainly wasn't cunning, so that's a generous description. I had the crazy idea
that if Mum and Dad actually *saw* Trixie, and understood
she was the size of a cockroach, but slightly cuter, their res-
ervations about adopting her as a pet would magically disappear. That was assuming Trixie didn't dump a loaf on the
kitchen floor (her bowels played up, I knew, when she was
stressed) or try to bite Dad on the grounds that he's big and
therefore asking for it.

"Nothing ventured, nothing gained" was my motto.

But before taking her home, I wanted to give her a couple

of circuits round the park, so she would be tired and therefore (maybe) better-behaved than normal.

It wasn't my intention to run into Destry Camberwick. It just happened that way.

I sat at a park bench, watching people pass. It amuses me sometimes to people-watch; I guess their occupations—that one looks like a teacher, or maybe a bank worker. That one is almost certainly a nurse. I could make up entire stories around them. She was returning home to her partner who'd been critical of her dress sense, and the steely glint in her eye spoke volumes; she'd had enough and was giving him the old heave-ho. That man was going back to a lonely house, a microwave meal, and an evening of watching *The Bachelor*.

Okay. Stop being judgmental. We're *all* weird in some way or other.

I think.

"Hello, Rob."

I looked up. It was Destry Camberwick and she wasn't alone. The Hound of the Baskervilles hunched at her side, glancing down at Trixie and drooling slightly. For once, Trixie was not frothing at the mouth with hatred. Maybe she'd woken up and smelled the canine coffee. Maybe she was just tired of being macho.

Destry Camberwick wasn't alone, but Destry Camberwick and her dog weren't alone either. A boy stood next to her; a boy I didn't recognize from school, and I know nearly everyone enrolled at Milltown, by sight if not by name. He was good-looking in a way that everyone would recognize, regardless of gender. Girls would *say* he was gorgeous. Boys would *know* he was gorgeous even if they wouldn't say it out loud.

"Hi," I said. Even in pressure situations, Rob Fitzgerald finds exactly the right word.

"How are you?" she said.

"Good. And you?" I don't think I'd ever hit such heights of brilliant conversation. It should be on YouTube.

"This is Justin," she said, indicating the piece of gor-geousness next to her. "Justin, this is Rob. We're at school together."

I stood and shook Justin by the hand. Justin? Of course his name was Justin. I'd bet his last name was some-thing double-barreled. Justin Freakin-Thyme or Justin A-Different-League.

"Pleased to meet you," I said.

"Likewise," he said. "Destry has told me a lot about you." He turned to Destry. "This *is* the Rob you've been going on about?"

Destry smiled. "The very one."

Why would Destry talk about me, especially to gorgeous Justin? You'd think they'd spend all their time gazing into gorgeous eyes, locking gorgeous lips, wrapped up in their own gorgeousness. It was a mystery. Luckily, Justin demys-tified it quickly.

"Destry told me about your cafeteria protest," he said. "That's great. Standing up for what you believe in. Suspended, right?" I nodded. "And then something about a talent contest and you gave this really individual performance."

I was starting to like Justin, despite the fact that he obviously liked Destry.

"What else?" He turned to Destry.

"Rob is a brilliant goalkeeper, it seems," she said. "I missed the game, but I heard all about it."

I shrugged in what I think was a hopeless attempt at modesty. I could feel myself blushing.

"It's great to meet you," said Justin.

"Yeah," said Destry. "We've got to go. See you Monday, yeah?"

"Sure," I said. And then I couldn't resist it. Maybe my ego was so stoked, I had to fan it some more. "Maybe I'll see you guys tomorrow if you happen to be walking down Mitchell Street at midday." I tried for a casual tone and then upped the stakes into a dramatic pause. "I'll be the one chained to the railings," I added.

Mum and Dad didn't fall in love with Trixie.

But they didn't hate her either.

She didn't try to rip Dad's throat out and she didn't take a dump on the kitchen floor. These were huge bonuses and, all in all, I was pleased.

Dad watched as she sniffed around the kitchen. He rubbed his chin.

"She *could* be a useful addition to the household," he said.

My heart leaped.

"Are you serious?" I said. "As a guard dog?"

"No," said Dad. "But you could stick your hand up her butt and she'd make a great oven glove."

I hate Dad sometimes.

"That's animal cruelty," I sniffed.

"Grandad?" I said. I'd dropped Trixie off at Agnes's apartment and then popped in to see him before I went home for dinner.

He grunted.

"I'm protesting animal cruelty in the town center tomorrow."

I'm not sure why I told him. I hadn't intended to. But I was inexperienced in these matters—Pop wasn't. I suspected he'd been involved in countless protests on issues of conscience. I don't know why I thought this either. When it comes to discussing his past, Grandad is tighter than an octopus's butthole. But I felt better after I told him.

"When?" he said.

"Twelve noon. Outside the supermarket."

"I'll be there," he said.

I knew he would.

53

ANDREW WAS PLEASED OUR PROTEST HAD BEEN PUT back to midday. He pointed out that, like the reporter, he enjoyed sleeping late on the weekends.

"But you *would* have turned up at nine o'clock, though?" I asked.

"Of course," he said. He gave me a small glare as if mortally offended that I'd doubted him. "Unless I'd still been asleep," he added. "Which I probably would've been."

We met at eleven thirty in a park close to the shopping mall. I'd made a detour to the newspaper office, but the place was locked up tight. I regretted not getting the reporter's phone number yesterday, but he probably wouldn't have given it to me anyway. I just hoped he remembered. Anyway, this wasn't really about getting onto the front page of the paper, I reminded myself, but getting publicity for the ill-treatment of animals at the slaughterhouse and exposing local businesses' lack of concern at how their meat was sourced. Yes, getting in the paper would achieve the challenge, but ultimately this wasn't about me.

Andrew was already sitting on a bench, a huge rucksack on the ground next to him. He looked pale and sweaty.

"Mate," I said. "You look pale and sweaty."

"Not surprising," he replied, a little breathless. "Do you have any idea how heavy this thing is?" He nodded down at the rucksack.

I didn't and acknowledged this freely. But, in solidarity, I tried to lift it and nearly dislocated my shoulder blade. Possibly both of them.

"What have you got in there?" I said. "An anvil or a life-sized bronze of an overweight hippo? Or both?"

"The equipment," said Andrew.

We'd discussed this last night. To chain yourself to railings you needed two things, we'd agreed. Railings and chains. We trusted the railings would be provided for us—it was staggeringly unlikely, we figured, that council workers would dismantle them from the front of the shopping mall during the night. That left chains. Neither Andrew nor I could afford to buy them, so this meant we had to raid parental sheds. Not stealing, naturally, but borrowing. We'd bring them back. I say "parental sheds," but really there was only one shed worth checking out.

My father works in real estate and doesn't own a hammer.

Our shed is bare. Or it would be if we actually had one.

Andrew's dad has a fluorescent vest and more power tools than Home Depot, and his shed is crammed with enough material to build a six-lane highway.

"Chains," I said.

"And padlocks," said Andrew. "You can't tie knots in chains. Well, not secure ones."

We sat there for twenty minutes, partly to let Andrew get his breath back and partly because we had a specific appointment for twelve.

"Destry has a boyfriend," I said.

"Yeah, I know," said Andrew. "Good-looking guy. He's just started at St. Martin's."

"Why didn't you tell me?"

"Why would I tell you?"

I spread my arms toward the sky and rolled my eyes. Slightly overdramatic, I admit, but also pointless, since Andrew was gazing at his sneakers as if they held important secrets.

"Hello, Andrew?" I said. "You know I'm in love with Destry Camberwick, and you didn't think to tell me of one slight problem? That she has a boyfriend who makes me look like Shrek?"

"He *doesn't* make you look like Shrek."

"Really?"

"No. You do that by yourself." Andrew got up and stretched. He looked at the rucksack and waved a hand at it. "Your turn," he added. "And, Rob, I didn't tell you about Destry's squeeze because it makes no difference."

I managed to get the rucksack up onto the bench, and then I crouched and slipped my arms through the straps. Standing straight was a problem, and for a second I had an image of toppling forward, the rucksack crushing me like a cockroach. When they lifted it off me, all that would remain would be a bloody stain on the grass. But I managed to stand, although I staggered a few paces.

"No difference?" I said. Andrew was crazy and this was proof.

"None," he said. "You'll never get anywhere if you have this negative attitude toward things, Rob. It's your biggest problem. You think you're unworthy of Destry and therefore you always will be. Have confidence. If you have confidence, then no one can compete with you. No boyfriend, no matter how good-looking, would stand a chance against you."

I must admit, his words made me feel good. Until I remembered.

"You said I look like Shrek," I said.

"You said you look like Shrek," he replied. "I was just agreeing with your own judgment. Don't complain that I'm dissing you, when all the time it's you talking yourself down."

Sometimes, Andrew is too smart for his own good. I may have said this before.

54

"I'M NOT TOTALLY STUPID, GRANDAD," I SAID.

Pop set up the chessboard and said nothing. When all the pieces were aligned, he regarded me across the board, one eye partially closed, like a strange and disturbing wink.

"I never thought you were *totally* stupid, young Rob. Just *partly* stupid, like the rest of humanity." He put a hand out, palm raised, inviting me to start. I moved my king's knight's pawn forward one square.

"Good example," he said. "What kind of dumb opening move is that?"

"One I've never tried before," I replied. "All the others have led to defeat."

"And you think this won't?" said Grandad.

"Oh, it probably will," I said. "But at least I will have found a *different* way to lose."

Grandad grunted and moved his king's pawn forward two spaces.

"I think you were either conscripted or volunteered for the Vietnam War in the mid-1960s," I said. "I believe you fought in that war, possibly at the Battle of Long Tan in 1966. Then you returned to Australia and met my grandmother in 1967. Maybe you were injured in the war. Or maybe you were simply allowed to come home. Am I close?" I moved my queen's knight's pawn forward two spaces. "I looked up wars in the 1960s," I added. "Ones involving Australians."

Grandad was silent. I tried not to meet his eyes, but I couldn't help noticing that his right hand shook slightly. I resisted the urge to fill the silence.

"I told you I don't want to talk about it," said Grandad finally. "Is that really too much to ask?"

"Yes," I said. "It is. Now, I'm not asking for all the *details*, the things you saw, the horrors I imagine you witnessed. I just want some *facts*, Grandad. That's all. Nice, uncomplicated facts about where you were. That can't be difficult, can it? 'Yes, I was in the Vietnam War. From 1965 to 1967. Okay, Rob? Fancy a cup of tea?' I'd be satisfied with that." I wasn't sure if that was strictly true, but Grandad didn't need to know it.

Pop stood and picked up his cane. He walked a few steps to the French windows and gazed out to the distant lake. Suddenly I was worried. Grandad never walked away from a chess game. Had I really touched a nerve I had no right to touch, simply to satisfy personal curiosity? Or was this a legitimate opportunity to fill in the gaps of my own background, my rightful inheritance?

Grandad sighed.

"Maybe you're right, Rob," he said. His voice was so low, I had to strain to catch the words. "Yes, I fought in the Vietnam War. I was stationed at Nui Dat in the province of Phuoc Tuy. Yes, I saw horrors, particularly at the Battle of Long Tan. And most of the horrors, I committed myself. Is that what you wanted to hear? Am I excused now?"

My mouth had gone dry. It wasn't so much the words Grandad used, as the tone. Not resigned—that's not quite right. But . . . weary. So weary.

"Pop," I said. "I'm sorry. I shouldn't pry. You're right. It's none of my business."

I wanted to get up and put a hand on his shoulder. No. I wanted to get up and hug him. But I was scared of what might happen next. What if he shuddered and pushed me away?

Pop stood against the bright backdrop of the window. Outside, the sun was falling toward the tops of the trees, and the distant waters of the lake were kissed by gold. Grandad *did* shudder then. And he seemed to shrink in on himself. When he turned to face me, it was as if he'd aged years in the last two minutes.

"Let's play," he said. Was it my imagination, or were his steps back to the table more unsteady than normal? He sat and gazed at the board, moved a piece forward. Then he met my eyes. "Not your fault, Rob," he said. He smiled, but it was twisted somehow. "Not remotely your fault, okay?"

I nodded, but that didn't mean I agreed with his words. I felt soaked in guilt.

"Sometimes," he said. "Sometimes, when you uncork a bottle and let the contents out, you can't get them back in. Do you know what I mean?"

I nodded again.

"I'll tell you something about my time in Vietnam," he said, "because I think you deserve to know why your grandmother couldn't stay with me. That part *is* your heritage and I guess you should know why you never had a grandma telling you bedtime stories, watching you grow up. But I won't talk about it too much, and when I'm done, I'm done, okay?"

I nodded.

He pointed to the board. "Your move," he said.

55

NOT ONLY HAD ANDREW BROUGHT ENOUGH STUFF TO chain us both to the supermarket's railings, but he'd brought enough to chain the staff and all of the customers as well. Not just chains, but padlocks, too. Small ones, enormous ones, over thirty in total. I found it hard to believe his dad would need so much material, even if he was a tradesman (which he was). Maybe he collected chains and padlocks like other people collect china figurines and antique snuffboxes. That was a weird thought, and I liked it.

Andrew saw to me first. I sat on the sidewalk up against the railings, and he wound the links through my arms and legs, across my neck, and through the bars of the railing. Occasionally he put in a padlock and locked it. We'd talked about this: if the butcher or the supermarket manager came out, we didn't want them unraveling the chains in five seconds and telling us to clear off. What kind of a protest would that be? No. We were here for the long term. A few passersby glanced our way, somewhat puzzled, but no one challenged us.

"How does that feel?" said Andrew when he was done. I flexed my arms and legs, tried to shift my butt across the sidewalk. All good. I was trussed like a Christmas turkey. (No. Animal cruelty. I was trussed like a Christmas nut loaf. No. That doesn't make sense.)

"Great," I said. "I'm not going anywhere."

"Okay," said Andrew. "My turn."

It was only then that we realized the problem. Andrew stood with a couple of miles of heavy-duty chain draped across his arms. He couldn't tie himself up, and I was in no position, since I could barely move the fingers on one hand.

"You could ask a passerby," I suggested.

He did, but it didn't work. Maybe that wasn't so surprising. *Excuse me. I'm fourteen years old and would much appreciate it if you'd lock me to this railing with lengths of chain and numerous padlocks.*

Luckily, Grandad turned up right at midday.

"G'day, guys," he said. "Need a hand?" He summed up the situation quickly. "I don't know," he mumbled. "If your brains were dynamite, you wouldn't have enough to blow your hats off."

"We're not wearing hats, Mr. F," Andrew pointed out.

Grandad quickly and efficiently shackled Andrew next to me. It must have been a bizarre spectacle for anyone paying attention—an old guy tying up a boy in the center of town. You can probably get arrested for that kind of thing. Luckily, no police came by. Plenty of other people did, but no one intervened, which, in a sense, was a real worry. We could've been holding up a jeweler's shop, and people would undoubtedly have strolled by, heads over their phones, chained and padlocked to their own interior set of railings. Had people always been like this? I thought not. I resolved to ask Grandad at some point. He wouldn't know *all* history but he'd lived through a fair portion of it.

"Okay," said Grandad, tugging at the padlocks and chains. He appeared satisfied that they were secure. "Comfortable?"

How can you be comfortable chained and padlocked to railings while the cold from the concrete creeps up your butt?

"Great, thanks," we both said together.

"And where are your signs?"

Andrew and I looked at each other. Correction. We *tried* to look at each other, but the chains were so tight, it was hard to make eye contact.

"You said you'd get the signs, Rob," said Andrew.

"No, I didn't."

"Well, you *should* have said it. I brought the chains and padlocks, after all. You can't expect me to do everything."

"Now, wait a moment . . ."

"Shut up," said Grandad. "You moronic mounds of cat poo." I was going to complain about the insults, but reckoned if I did, Grandad might gag both of us and then walk away. "So here you are, chained to railings, but no one knows why. Brilliant! Were you relying on telepathy or simply hoping people will ask you? 'Excuse me, but are you chained up for a reason or is this how teenagers now spend their weekends?' I wouldn't talk to you. I'd pretend you didn't exist, just like all these people are doing." Grandad waved a hand to encompass the surroundings. The town center was busy now, but no one was looking in our direction. Part of the problem was that we were both close to the ground, being chained to the railings and all, so it was difficult for anyone to spot us. Grandad sighed. "I'll go and get some cardboard and markers," he said. Now he shook his head. "Honest to God. You guys are meant to be the future of the human race. Heaven help us all! Okay. I'll be quick. Don't go anywhere."

"We can't, Mr.—"

"He's joking, Andrew," I said.

"Oh."

Pop was only gone ten minutes, but in that time Destry Camberwick showed up.

"Hi, Rob. Hey, Andrew," said Destry.

"Destry. How's it going?" said Andrew.

"Good." She squatted down so we could see her more easily, rather than staring at her kneecaps. Don't get me wrong. I *liked* staring at her kneecaps. They were brilliant kneecaps. But it was also great to look into her eyes. "Now, I know it's rude to ask," she said, "but I couldn't help noticing you're chained to the railings." She put a hand on *my* knee, and a part of me shriveled and died. "Just as you said, Rob. But is there a reason? Or is this how you guys like to spend your weekend?"

I explained.

"You need signs," she said when I was done.

"I know," I replied. "My grandfather has just gone to get some. Oh, here he is."

Pop had not only brought the stuff to make the signs. He'd also written on them and attached them to poles.

> Boycott Meat at Dixon's the Butcher and
> Morgan's Supermarket.
> Don't Support Animal Cruelty!

He propped them between our knees.

"Grandad," I said. "This is Destry Camberwick."

Pop looked at Destry and then back at me. At that moment I regretted introducing him; I should've known better. I should've said, *I have no idea who this old fart is, Destry.* That wouldn't have worked but it might have bought me some time.

"What? *The* Destry Camberwick?"

"Er. Well. *A* Destry Camberwick," I said.

"The one you're in love with?" asked Pop.

There was silence for two months. Okay, not two months,

probably more like five seconds, but certainly plenty of time to die a couple of hundred times.

"No," I said after two months. "That's another Destry Camberwick entirely."

You can hope for the earth to swallow you, but let's face it, it's unlikely to happen. Especially when you're chained to a supermarket's railings with a sign clenched between your thighs. There's probably some law of physics involved.

Grandad looked Destry up and down.

"I thought you were an eighties rock band," he said.

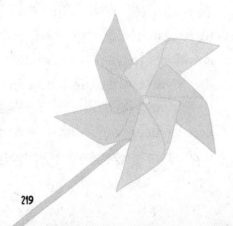

56

THERE WAS ONCE A DOG WHO LIVED IN THE 1920S, somewhere in America.

He was a well-loved dog, so well loved that when the family went on vacation, they didn't hire a house sitter or put him in a boarding kennel. They'd miss him too much.

So they took the dog with them on a very long road trip. A very, very long road trip.

All would have been fine, except one day their dog went missing. The family was horrified and upset. They searched and searched but couldn't find him. Eventually, they had to return home. They had no choice. It was a long and emotional journey back. Many tears were shed; they knew they'd never see their dog again.

Except—yes, it's happened before and it will probably keep on happening—the dog found his way home. Imagine how happy the family was to see him limp up their driveway a few months after they'd got back. Imagine their surprise as well.

You see, the dog had walked two and a half thousand miles to get home.

Do you know any person who would walk twenty-five hundred miles for someone they love?

Speaking of dogs . . .

There was once a dog called Hachiko and he lived in Japan. The person he shared a life with was Hidesaburo Ueno, a lecturer at the University of Tokyo. Every day, Hidesaburo would go off to work, and every evening, he would return to Shibuya Station on the train.

Hachiko would always be there at the station waiting for him. *Always.* And they would be so happy to see each other.

But one day, Hidesaburo died. He died at work, but of course Hachiko didn't know that. So he waited at the station as he had always done. When his master didn't arrive (or is "master" the right word? Is "friend" better?), he wondered what had happened. But he knew that if he waited, Hidesaburo would turn up eventually. That was the way it had always worked. So he waited and he waited.

Every day for over nine years.

When Hachiko died, the people of Tokyo put up a statue of him. The statue is still there at Shibuya Station in Tokyo. So, in a sense, Hachiko is still waiting.

57

FOR THE FIRST HALF HOUR OF OUR PROTEST, WE WERE basically invisible. But then things changed.

First of all, the butcher came out. Someone must have told him we were chained up and protesting against his shop, because he was suddenly in our faces and not happy.

"What the blankety hell do you kids think you're doing?" he yelled.

"Don't you blankety swear at these blankety children," yelled Grandad. "They are doing what is only fair and reasonable—protesting about how you get your meat from a slaughterhouse that treats animals cruelly. How the steaks and sausages you sell were once living creatures whose throats were cut, without anesthetic, without even being stunned properly. YOU ARE MAKING A LIVING OUT OF SUFFERING."

The butcher glanced around. Most passersby had stopped

to listen. It obviously occurred to him that this was not the best publicity for his shop, because he lowered his voice and took a step toward Grandad.

"Look, mate," he muttered. "I don't have any choice where I get my meat from. There's only one slaughterhouse around here and—"

"No excuses," said Pop. He raised his voice even more. "Go back to your shop and keep your inhumane trade going. There's blood on your hands, mate. There's BLOOD ON YOUR HANDS!"

The butcher glanced down.

"Of course there is," he said. "I'm a butcher."

"HE ADMITS IT," yelled Grandad.

"I'm calling the police," said the butcher. He started backing away toward his shop.

"HE'S CALLING THE POLICE ON THESE CHILDREN WHO ARE ONLY TRYING TO PROTECT INNOCENT ANIMALS!"

A few members of the crowd snarled at the guy as he scuttled out of sight. I almost felt sorry for him.

"I need a wee, Andrew," I said. I figured I could get home and back in no more than fifteen minutes. "Give Pop the keys to the padlocks."

"What keys?" said Andrew.

"Tell me you brought keys as well as padlocks."

"No. Chains and padlocks. That's all we discussed."

"Oh, great," I said. I tried to clench my legs together but, what with the chains, it was difficult.

Grandad ambled off around two o'clock to get himself a vegetable pie. I was really thirsty but my bladder didn't need anything else. I was hungry as well, but I didn't want to tempt fate, so I turned down his offer to get me something to eat or drink.

"Wanna fight?" came a familiar voice. "C'mon, Fitzgerald. Man up. Or has the cat got yer tongue?"

It was possible Daniel Smith had been watching for the last hour, waiting for his chance, because Grandad had been gone no longer than two minutes.

"How can I fight you, Daniel?" I said. "I'm chained to a railing."

"Always an excuse not to man up," said Daniel. "I should kick your head in right now."

"Do that," said Andrew, "and you'll regret it the rest of your life. All ten minutes of it."

"Hello, Daniel Smith," said Miss Pritchett.

"Oh God," said Daniel.

"Miss?" I said. "Is there any truth in the rumor you're a superhero with powers beyond the dreams of mortals?"

Miss Pritchett read the signs.

"I should, to be fair," she said, "tell you that the principal is having a cup of tea and an iced bun in a cafe just down the road. I suspect she'll stumble across you in less than half an hour, and you know what she thinks about bringing our school into disrepute."

"We can't go yet, Miss," I said. "The reporter hasn't turned up."

"And we're protesting about animal cruelty," Andrew added. "How is that bringing the school into disrepute?"

"Ah," said Miss Pritchett. "You might think that's a sweet and fitting thing to do. *I* might think it's a sweet and fitting thing to do. But that's not to say *everyone* will see it that way . . ."

Sweet and fitting . . .

58

"**IT WAS AUGUST 1966,**" **SAID GRANDAD.** "**I WAS** stationed at Nui Dat, like I told you."

He picked up a pawn, thought better of it, and replaced it on the board.

"I was twenty-seven," he said. "An old man compared to some of the kids who were there. I'd volunteered, but others had been drafted. Their birthdays came up in the lottery." He looked at me, saw confusion in my eyes. "The government ran a kind of lottery. Three hundred and sixty-five days went into a barrel. If your birthday was pulled out . . ." He shrugged. "Happy blankety birthday."

"*Why* did you volunteer, Grandad?" I asked.

"The Old Lie," he replied. "Have you done Wilfred Owen in school yet?" I shook my head. "*Dulce et decorum est, pro patria mori*. Latin for 'It's sweet and fitting to die for your country.' That's the Old Lie. And that's what

Owen turned into the most beautiful antiwar poetry."

"But why is it a lie? Isn't it a good thing to fight for your country, for freedom . . . ?"

Pop held up a hand.

"I'm not going to argue with you on this, Rob," he said. "That's a question you have to work out for yourself. I'm just telling you *my* experience. I saw many deaths." For a moment his eyes changed, as if focusing on a point in his past. "Many, many deaths. None of them were good. None of them were noble. . . ."

His voice trailed off. I waited but the silence stretched.

"You were stationed at Nui Dat," I prompted.

Grandad gave a small shudder, and then he was back in the room with me. He smiled and moved his king's knight. That looked like a mistake to me, but then, he'd made moves before that seemed like mistakes and turned out to be no such thing. I tried to focus on the positions on the board.

"We came under fire from the Vietcong. You know who the Vietcong were?" Again, I shook my head. "They were communist soldiers who fought alongside the North Vietnamese army. Australian troops, along with soldiers from America and some other allied nations like New Zealand, fought for South Vietnam against the north and the Vietcong."

"Why?"

"For the same reason *all* wars are fought. An idea," said Grandad. "In this case, the idea that communism was a bad,

bad thing, that it was spreading across the globe and would destroy the Western World's way of life. Basically, it was America's war, but we got dragged in."

"Was that idea an old lie?"

Grandad shook his head. "Read about it, young Rob. I told you, you have to make up your own mind about things like communism versus capitalism. I *thought* I was telling you a story. Do you want to hear it or not? Because, trust me, I'm happy not to revisit this part of my life."

I moved my bishop.

"Sorry," I said. "Go on."

"We were ordered to track down the Vietcong who'd fired on us. You have to understand, this war was very different from other wars. For one thing, much of it was jungle warfare. The Vietcong knew the jungle. It was their home. For us, it was alien and confusing. So we heard the shots, but we didn't know where the enemy had gone. We left our compound, one hundred and eight of us, and went searching for them. We ended up in a place called Long Tan."

He stopped again, reached for his queen's rook. I saw that his hands were shaking, and I regretted putting pressure on him to talk. But it was too late. I think I knew that. For good or bad, this story was going to come out.

"The thing is," said Grandad, "we thought *we* were tracking the Vietcong, but in reality, they'd been tracking us. One hundred and eight soldiers, young men not much older than you, Rob, not really . . . surrounded by an army that didn't take prisoners. Trapped in a space no bigger than two football fields. Surrounded."

"How many enemy soldiers were there, Grandad?"

"Oh," he said. He moved his rook halfway down the board. "No one's sure. But probably two and a half thousand. Two and a half thousand against one hundred and eight. What do you think about those odds?"

I couldn't say anything.

"We knew we were going to die," said Grandad. I'd never heard his voice so soft. "It was the strangest feeling."

59

GRANDAD, DANIEL SMITH, DESTRY CAMBERWICK, MISS
Pritchett, and the local butcher (soon to be followed by the
principal). My social life had never been so busy. I should
chain myself to railings more often.

And the guest appearances kept on coming.

"Hello, Mum. Hello, Dad," I said. I didn't really have a
choice. They stood in front of me, hands on hips, glaring
down with looks that might well kill, given enough time. At
that moment they just made me feel queasy. "Fancy seeing
you here! Doing some shopping? Best to avoid the butcher
and the supermarket, in my humble opinion . . ." I tried a
winning smile.

"What on earth are you doing?" said Mum. Every word
was a dagger. Between the words and the looks, I was dead
meat—which was ironic, under the circumstances.

"Well, I'm chained to a railing, protesting animal cruelty,"

I said. "I thought that might have been obvious from the chains and the signs."

"Are you being a smart aleck again?"

"Look . . . ," said Grandad. It wasn't, as it turned out, a wise thing to say. I don't know why. "Look" is not a very provocative word. Mum spun to face him.

"I might have known *you'd* be involved," she spat. "Whenever Rob gets into trouble, you're around."

Dad put his hand on Mum's arm, but she shook it off.

"You're a bad influence," she continued, her eyes boring into Grandad's.

"Thanks," said Pop. "I appreciate the compliment. It's good to know I can still *be* a bad influence."

"And as for you . . ." Mum returned her attention to me. That was a pity. I was enjoying Grandad coming under fire for a while and giving me a well-earned break. "You are grounded."

I was tempted to tell her this was indeed true because I couldn't actually get *off* the ground, but, wisely I feel, I kept my mouth shut.

"You are grounded," she said, "for the rest of your life. Now get up. You're coming home."

"Ah," I said. "Bit of a problem there, actually."

Andrew explained about the oversight regarding keys to padlocks. Mum rolled her eyes.

"You kids are idiots," she said.

"I told them . . . ," said Grandad.

"Shut up," said Mum. She pointed a finger at Andrew. He flinched. "Call your father and get him to unlock you," she said. She turned the finger on me. I couldn't help it; I flinched too. "I expect you home in no more than half an hour," she said. "Otherwise, your punishment will be extended."

What? Grounded not just for life, but the afterlife as well? I didn't say this. I was scared just *thinking* it.

Grandad, Daniel Smith, Destry Camberwick, Miss Pritchett, the local butcher, Mum, Dad, and Miss Cunningham.

"I want to see you in my office first thing on Monday morning," she roared. Or maybe it was a bellow.

"Yes, Miss Cunningham," Andrew and I murmured.

Grandad opened his mouth to speak. The principal cringed and beat a hasty retreat.

Things were going brilliantly. All this trouble and the reporter hadn't even turned up. It couldn't get worse.

Then it got worse.

Grandad, Daniel Smith, Destry Camberwick, Miss Pritchett, Mum, Dad, the butcher, Miss Cunningham, and the police.

Hurrah!

"What's going on here?" There were two police officers. One was female and one wasn't. Neither appeared particularly friendly. Then again, I couldn't help but stare at their guns, which didn't radiate goodwill and peace on earth.

"Umm . . . ," I said, proving once again that under pressure I always find exactly the right words.

"These kids are protesting against animal cruelty," said Grandad. "They're drawing attention to the fact that local businesses are profiting from immoral practices."

"Is that right?" said the male officer. He drew himself up straight and sort of thrust his chest toward Pop. "Is that right?"

"Yes," said Grandad. "And yes to your second question as well."

"Are you trying to be smart? Are you? Are you trying to be smart?"

"They're not breaking any laws," said Grandad.

"Oh, aren't they? Aren't they?" said the officer. "I guess I should be the judge of that. I say, I'm the one who should be judging."

"Why do you say everything twice?" said Grandad. "Have you got a learning difficulty? I said, have you got a learning difficulty?"

I'm not sure what would have happened to us if the police hadn't suddenly become more interested in Grandad than Andrew and me. I can't imagine they would have arrested us, but it was academic anyway, because when the male officer took a step forward, Grandad punched him in the face.

By an amazing stroke of luck, this happened to be when the reporter turned up. He got a great shot of us chained to the railings, the signs prominent. He also got a brilliant shot of Grandad punching a police officer in the face, and of Pop being bundled into the back of a police car. Suddenly, disaster was averted.

Except for Grandad, of course.

Grandad, Daniel Smith, Destry Camberwick, Miss Pritchett, Mum, Dad, the butcher, Miss Cunningham, the police, the reporter, and Andrew's dad.

He didn't have the keys to the padlocks, so he had to go home for a power tool and cut us free.

He wasn't happy either. He'd have to join the end of a very long line, but I didn't tell him that.

60

CONSEQUENCES.

Aren't there always consequences? Life would be much better if we could just get rid of them. Anyway, here are a few:

Grandad was released without charge. The police were very good about it, because although Grandad was older than God's dog, he *had* assaulted an officer. He *had* broken the law. Maybe the police figured it wouldn't be good for public relations to charge a really old guy with assault. Maybe they just decided to cut him some slack. Whatever the reason, he was home a few hours later.

(I knew what had really happened. Pop had bought me and Andrew some time. He'd hit the officer so they'd be more concerned with him and leave us alone. I asked Grandad about this and he snorted. "Don't kid yourselves," he said. "And don't make assumptions. My actions are my responsibility. Just as yours are yours. And never, *never* disrespect the police," he added. "They do a fantastic job under trying circumstances." I was going to point out that I *do* respect the police and that it was Grandad who'd punched one of them, but I let it go.)

I made the front page of the newspaper. They spelled my name wrong, but that didn't matter. (How could they spell "Rob" wrong?) They also had a photo of Grandad being taken away. Surprisingly, our protest reawakened interest in conditions at the slaughterhouse. A few people wrote to the paper and expressed support for a meat boycott. This, in turn, prompted the butcher and the supermarket to announce that they'd no longer source meat from the slaughterhouse until there was an ironclad assurance that humane practices were being used *all* the time.

Humane practices *were* established in the local slaughterhouse. Closed-circuit television cameras were installed, and every part of the operation was open to scrutiny.

I got a text message:

Congratulations, Rob. You met the challenge. Expect another one soon.

I replied, Thanks, Grandad. Looking forward to it.

I got another message. **Not your grandfather.**

I wasn't, of course, buying that.

Miss Cunningham wanted to suspend us for at least three days, but she couldn't. I think someone pointed out that after school hours, we could pretty much do what we wanted. We hadn't been wearing our school uniforms and therefore couldn't be accused of bringing the institution into disrepute. She wasn't happy and I knew our school lives had just been made much trickier. But we could go to school and I was glad.

Mum and Dad grounded me, as they'd promised, not just for life but all eternity. Well, okay, a week. It felt like eternity. The following Saturday I turned up at the Old Farts' Palace, took Trixie for a walk in the park, and visited Grandad for a game of chess.

61

"WE THOUGHT WE WERE IN HELL," SAID GRANDAD.
"Especially when the monsoon storm hit."

"A storm?"

"Yeah. Stroke of luck, that, huh? One hundred and eight very scared soldiers, surrounded by thousands of enemies, and the skies opened. Lightning everywhere, huge claps of thunder, and torrential rain that reduced visibility almost to zero." Grandad gave a small and rueful smile. "Absolutely the worst time to become effectively blind."

"What did you do?"

"What do you think we did? None of us could see very well, but we fired at them and they fired at us. Australians, a few Kiwis, and thousands of Vietcong all making the required moves in that stupid dance called war." Pop took my knight with his bishop. I'd expected that and took his bishop with my queen.

"Check," I said.

Grandad rubbed at the stubble on his chin as he gazed at the board.

"The battle lasted three and a half hours, though for us it seemed an eternity. Someone a long time afterward reckoned about four hundred thousand rounds of ammunition were fired. Four hundred thousand! That's almost beyond belief." Pop moved his king back a space. "Nearly two thousand shots a minute. Thirty a second. Some soldiers passed out because of cordite fumes from the guns. Imagine it. A ferocious tropical storm, blinding rain, thunder you couldn't hear because of the deafening gunfire, brilliant flashes of lightning that sometimes showed you the enemy advancing. Always advancing. I've had plenty of nightmares in my time. None compared to that waking one."

I knew my next move but didn't make it. Grandad was wandering through the jungle of his memory and I had to wait until he returned.

"Here's something strange," he said. "The enemy soldiers kept coming toward us. Always advancing. But they didn't try to hide from our fire. They didn't take shelter behind trees or bushes, though God knows there were plenty of them. No. Have you ever seen a zombie movie, Rob?"

I hadn't, but I'd seen a television show about them once when Mum and Dad were out. I nodded.

"They were like that." He gave the smallest of shudders. "They came toward us, we shot them, and they went down.

Then two more would take the place of the fallen. We'd shoot them, and more would take their place. It was the most bizarre thing. All that, for hours and hours, in the lightning and the rain and the clouds of gun smoke. Afterward, we found something like two hundred and fifty Vietcong bodies, but we killed and wounded many more than that."

"How many Australians died, Grandad?" I asked.

"Eighteen," he said. "And twenty-four wounded. I was one of them. Shot in the arm, and do you know, I hadn't realized until the battle was over. For all I know, I was shot in the first minute and then spent hours fighting. I remember looking down, seeing the bullet wound, and only then feeling pain." He shook his head as if disputing his own story. "I spent some time in a field hospital, before being shipped home to Australia. I never went to war again. Unfortunately, it didn't really matter because it turned out I brought the war back with me. Up here." He touched the side of his head with an index finger.

I didn't say anything. I thought I understood, and anyway I knew it was best to say as little as possible. Grandad glanced at the board.

"I think it's your move," he said.

I moved my queen to the farthest row.

"Checkmate," I said.

Grandad gave a start and then bent his head over the board. His eyes darted over the remaining pieces.

"Well, I'll be blanked," he said. "It is. Checkmate." He held his hand out over the board. "Congratulations," he said.

"Did you let me win?" I asked. I didn't take his hand.

"No," said Grandad. His voice was sharp. "I told you I'd never let you win and I didn't. You beat me fair and square, Rob."

"Do you swear?"

"I swear."

"Cross your heart and hope to die?"

"Cross my heart and hope to die."

I shook his hand.

We sat on our usual bench overlooking the lake and the dribbling fountain. Grandad had said he needed fresh air, so we'd put the chessboard away and ambled down the path. A sickly sun made small sparks on the water's surface.

"Post-traumatic stress disorder," I said.

"Ah," said Pop. "Yes. A real mouthful, that, but just about the long and short of it. Sometimes, when you go through a deeply distressing, painful experience, it can be difficult, maybe impossible, to shake it off. It stays with you, tormenting you long after the experience has ended."

"That's what you meant when you said you brought the war back with you?"

"Yes." Grandad leaned forward on the bench and put a hand across his chest. "I told you all this to explain about your grandmother, not because I wanted sympathy or to convince you war is awful. So. I'm going to finish this story now, Rob, and we won't talk about it again, okay?"

"Okay."

"I mentioned a poem by Wilfred Owen earlier. He fought in the First World War, just over a century ago. Now, there was a war that defied belief. Thousands and thousands of men slaughtered, routinely, to win a few yards of mud between the trenches. And the probability was that those few yards would be lost the next day." Grandad shook his head. "Soldiers suffered PTSD because they viewed horrors beyond imagining, day after day, month after month. But no one knew about post-traumatic stress disorder, so when men broke down screaming, the officers thought it was cowardice. They lined them up in front of a firing squad and shot them. As an example to others, you see."

Grandad leaned back on the bench.

"In that poem, '*dulce et Decorum Est*,' which, incidentally, you *must* read, Owen talked about watching someone die and he said, 'In all my dreams, before my helpless sight, He plunges at me, guttering, choking, drowning.' *In all my dreams, before my helpless sight*. That's it. That's it *exactly*, Rob. I tried to live a normal life when I got back to Sydney, but I couldn't. Because every time I slept, I saw the same scenes replayed over and over. Before my helpless sight."

I put my arm across his shoulders but I don't think he noticed.

"Bella tried to help, but she couldn't. I'd wake up scream-ing, covered in sweat, and she would hold me for hours until

I calmed down. Maybe she could have dealt with that, but the ghosts came during waking hours as well."

"Ghosts?" I said.

"The ghosts of those I'd killed. The ghosts of friends who'd died, not just in Long Tan but in other battles. They moved in with me. I still see them, Rob. God help me, I still see them from time to time." He wiped at his forehead, and his hand came away covered in a film of sweat. "They don't terrify me anymore. In fact, their company is more comforting than anything else. But your grandmother . . . well, she endured as long as she could, far longer than I had the right to expect. But the ghosts pushed her out. *I* pushed her out. It was the only way she could possibly survive."

A thin breeze cut across the lake and I shivered.

"Your grandmother didn't abandon me, Rob. She didn't abandon your father or you. That's something you need to know."

"So why didn't you tell me before, Grandad?"

He sighed.

"Because sometimes stories are just too sad, Rob. And too painful. But, you know something? I feel better for having told you. I really do."

I hugged him to me and we sat in silence for a few minutes.

"Oh, God, I'm sorry, Rob," said Grandad finally.

"What for, Pop?"

"For this. I didn't want it to happen like this, but I can't stop it. Forgive me, please."

"I have no idea what you're talking about, Pop."

Grandad gave a long, drawn-out sigh. His head lay on my shoulder. I waited for him to take another breath, but he didn't.

62

I LOST MY MIND FOR A FEW DAYS. BETWEEN GRANDAD'S death and his funeral—and I'm not sure how long that was—I lost my mind.

How can I explain? Words are so clunky and fall far short of the reality they're meant to represent. Long gaps of time. I'd find myself staring out the window, and Mum would be talking to me but I had no idea what she'd said. I had no interest in what she'd said. One time, I realized I was screaming at Mum and Dad but I can't remember why. I don't think I knew even then, but I remember the words.

"You don't understand. Why can't you blankety understand? I said to him, 'Cross your heart and hope to die.' And he said, 'Cross my heart and hope to die.' Get it? I invited this. Me. My fault. Why don't you understand?"

Mum had sometimes called my relationship with Grandad unhealthy, though I know she didn't mean it in a nasty way. What she was talking about was how, in the normal way of things, a thirteen-year-old would spend a *socially acceptable* amount of time with a grandfather, but the grandad wouldn't be a *friend*, wouldn't be someone a kid would seek out and talk to about personal things. Spending time with kids my own age would have been normal, not hanging around an old people's home. That's just weird.

I didn't go to school for a couple of weeks. I'd have probably been suspended, anyway, but I didn't go so it didn't matter. You see, Daniel Smith saw me a day or two after Grandad died. I have no idea why I was out on the streets. Maybe Mum and Dad had insisted I go with them somewhere. I also can't remember what Daniel said, but I can guess. Let's be honest, it's not difficult to predict what's going to come out of Daniel's mouth.

A tooth, it turned out. Because I punched him.

I'm not proud of this. Later I went to his house and apologized. He never bullied me again, but I don't know if that was because I punched him or because I apologized. Maybe it doesn't matter. Maybe it does. I'll think about it, but not right now.

Andrew was a good friend. I know this because he largely left me alone with my feelings. He'd come over after school and tell me stories of the school day. He sent Destry's love and I nodded and thanked him, and asked him to tell her I appreciated her concern. And I did. But here's something strange. Or maybe it isn't. All that love I'd felt for her, that churning feeling in my stomach, that sense of blood burning just to hear her name—well, all that hadn't died, exactly, but it somehow didn't seem important anymore. Destry was a stranger. Maybe she wouldn't be in the future. Maybe we could become friends. I hoped so, because she seemed like a nice person.

But not a lot mattered to me at that point.

Mum and Dad were, I think, really supportive. I'm sure I wasn't the easiest child to deal with at the time. And, of course, my dad had also lost his dad. Mum had lost her father-in-law. She'd often argued with Grandad, but I knew she loved him. I didn't give their feelings much thought, though. I was too wrapped up in my own grief to let anyone else's in.

In all my dreams, before my helpless sight.

But time passed. I ate, I slept (when the nightmares let me), and I read. Time passed.

Then it was the day of the funeral.

63

IT WAS THE FIRST TIME I WORE A SUIT. MUM AND DAD
took me to a shop in the town center, not a million miles from
where Andrew and I had chained ourselves to the railings.
Already that seemed like it had happened to a different
person in a different time.

A man in the shop measured me and promised Mum and
Dad that he could do the necessary alterations in time. They
didn't have much call for suits that would fit a thirteen-year-
old, and there wasn't time to tailor one from scratch, but
he had an idea of how to make separate elements—trousers
and jacket—work together.

He was as good as his word. I went to the shop the day
before the funeral, and the suit fit beautifully. He'd also
found a vest that matched and was the right size. I put on a
bright white shirt, and he knotted a red tie around my collar
and took me to a full-length mirror.

It was amazing. I gazed at myself, and it was like gazing at a stranger. I think it was the first time I'd smiled since Grandad's death. I studied my reflection and I knew he would have been proud of me.

On the morning of the funeral, Mum asked if I wanted to say a few words during the service. The question took me by surprise and my heart hammered.

Did I want to say a few words? Of course I did. What's more, I knew I *could* say a few words. If this had been only a few months previously, it would have been impossible. But my panic attacks were, for the time being at least, under control and my self-confidence high. All those challenges had brought me that confidence. But I shook my head.

"I don't think so, Mum," I said.

"Are you sure, Rob?" Mum ran a hand through my hair. "You might regret it afterward."

"Yeah, I might. But I think I'll just listen to what others say."

"You're certain?"

"This is not the right time for me," I said. I didn't know why I knew this, but I did. "When it is, I'll have my say."

I was stunned by the number of people who turned up to the funeral. I'm not sure what I'd been expecting, but I guess I must have assumed it would be just family, and maybe one or two people from the old folks' home.

The place was packed.

Mum, Dad, and I lined up at the entrance to the crematorium and welcomed the guests. Andrew was there, of course. Miss Cunningham came as well, which surprised me. I thought the principal would've hated Grandad, but it seems not. She told me she wanted to pay her respects to a man who was so passionate about my education.

Many of the old people from the home showed up, as well as ten or twelve staff. The place had organized a couple of buses. I recognized nearly all the home's tenants. I was pleased to see Jim wasn't there. I'm not sure I could've coped knowing someone who had no idea what day it was had been made to come. Grandad would've hated that as well. Agnes gave me a massive hug and shook Mum's and Dad's hands. A whole procession of old people came along, and all of them hugged me as if I was a long-lost friend. How strange is that?

There were also six people I didn't recognize. They were roughly Grandad's age, and a couple wore medals pinned to their chests. Each shook my hand and bowed their head as they entered. Vietnam vets. People who'd known Pop for over fifty years, who knew what he'd been through, because they'd been there with him. *Do they have their own ghosts?* I wondered. I imagined they did.

When everyone had taken their seats, the service began.

It didn't last long, because Grandad had been clear on what he wanted. More precisely, what he *didn't* want. God, for example, wasn't welcome, because Pop wasn't a fan of religion. No priest or vicar, because he didn't want some-one who'd never met him talking about what a great person he'd been. Instead, a number of people he'd known stood up at the front, next to the casket, and spoke.

Dad gave a moving speech. He made a few jokes and I even laughed at a couple. Two staff from the old people's home got up and said something. One wiped away a tear, but there weren't many tears. There were stories. Agnes stood, though she had to hold on to a rail for support. I wondered if she had any idea that Grandad had bet she'd die before him. Knowing Grandad, he'd probably told her. Agnes surprised me by saying that Pop had been the gen-tlest and kindest person she'd ever known. "He tried to hide that," she remarked. "He pretended to have a thick skin and to despise most people around him. Maybe he fooled some people, but he didn't fool me. Pat Fitzgerald was a softie, and I loved him for it."

She looked around the crematorium.

"I'll tell you one thing. He wouldn't be seen dead in a place like this." I couldn't help it. I burst out laughing, even though it wasn't the most original of jokes. A few other people did too. "He told me he wanted to be burned in a big barrel on the edge of the lake at home," she continued. "'Put a grill over the top, douse me with petrol, and cook up some sau-sages,' he said. I pointed out that there weren't many people, even in the Old Farts' Palace, who'd be prepared to eat a smoked sausage sandwich with his smell clinging to it. 'In this place,' he said, 'that would be a step up in dining experience.'"

Agnes caught my eye.

"I know he told Rob this," she said. I grinned and put a thumb up. "Rob, who he loved more than life itself. And Rob, who loved him. A strange couple, but one that made my life shine brighter, right toward its end. So thank you, Pat Fitzgerald, and thank you, Rob Fitzgerald. For brightening my life. And for brightening each other's."

I didn't cry then, but I came close. Grandad used to say I'd cry over a sick mosquito, I was the biggest wuss in the cosmos. But so far, I'd been strong.

That changed when one of the old men stood, pulled out a bugle, and played "The Last Post" as Grandad's coffin slid along a conveyor and through a pair of sliding doors.

I wasn't the only one who totally lost it.

It's a universal truth, so I've been told, that after a funeral people can't slink away home. They have to return to someone's house, eat stale ham sandwiches, and chat in low tones.

People came to our house, ate stale ham sandwiches, and chatted in low tones for a while. The Vietnam vets didn't, though. They melted away when the service was done. I guess when you've been through what they've been through, you can give ham sandwiches the middle finger if you want.

People came up to me and expressed their sorrow. I

thanked them and we were all very, very polite in our suits and our little murmuring clusters.

When my phone buzzed, I assumed it was Andrew. He'd gone home after the formalities, and I couldn't blame him. But it wasn't Andrew.

I have your last challenge for you, Rob, the text read. **Meet me in your back garden. Now. I'll give it to you personally. It's time we met, don't you think?**

64

I LOOSENED THE KNOT OF MY TIE AND UNDID THE TOP
button of my shirt. It wasn't hot, but I was slick with sweat.

I've read plenty of books, so I was familiar with the idea
of *moving as if in a dream*, but this was the first time I'd
done it. There was a drumming in my ears that made all
other noise recede to a distant hum. I was intensely aware
of being *inside* my body, looking out through the arch of my
brows. Despite that, I was surprised when I glanced down
toward the handle of our back door and saw my own right
hand reaching out to turn it.

You see, I'd spent so much time convincing myself it
was Grandad who'd sent the texts, that even now I couldn't
believe it wasn't. What would I do if I opened the door and
saw Pop standing on the lawn under the clothesline? Would
I scream? Or would I run and hug him? A drop of sweat
ran into my eyes, and the sting brought me back to myself. I

turned the handle and pushed the door open.

Agnes stood in the center of the lawn. She smiled, though it was a strange and twisted thing. She held up a cell phone.

I didn't smile. But I did walk and stand in front of her. The sky had turned gloomy, swollen clouds threatening rain, and the garden was dark and depressed.

"I need to explain," said Agnes.

"Yes," I said.

"This may take time. Do you want to go inside and sit down?"

"No," I said.

"You're upset," said Agnes.

"You think?" I said.

"I'm not sure how I should explain," said Agnes. "And you may not need to sit because you're young, but I do because I'm old." She pointed to a rain-stained bench close to a shriveled flower bed. I'd forgotten it was there. "Please, Rob?"

I have no idea how old Agnes is. Old. Grandad old. And I couldn't let her stand. But I was not happy. In fact, inside I was a coil of hard resentment and I couldn't even say why this was. So I shrugged and stalked off to the bench. She followed, but I didn't give her the comfort of my watching or pretending I cared. I vowed I would say nothing, that my silence would be the punishment she deserved.

Agnes put her handbag on the ground and was quiet for a while. I think she was catching her breath.

"I can't count the hours your grandfather and I spent

talking about you, Rob," she said finally. I looked at the grass beneath my feet. She sighed. "This is so hard," she murmured, more to herself than to me. "When you get old, something strange happens to your world. Even though, in your time, you've been to exotic places, had experiences that are wonderful, fought wars, met people you'll never forget—in short, had a marvelous and varied life, at the end everything narrows. For some people it becomes their home or, if they're lucky enough, their partner. Sometimes, the memory of a love now gone, a person who shone brightly but faded all too quickly." She wiped at her eyes as if her own words had struck a nerve. "In Pat's case, the world narrowed down to you, Rob. I'm not sure you need to know this. Maybe you don't. But *you* were his center, his sun, and he orbited you. He bathed in your warmth."

I could feel tears prickling, but I couldn't let them free. So I shut my eyes and bit my lip.

"It was your grandfather's idea to give you those challenges," she said. "This is very important, maybe not to you—I don't know—but to me. You must understand that in this whole business, I was merely the finger on the phone." She laughed. "Pat was rubbish with technology. You know that. The only reason I texted you those messages was because your grandad couldn't. I offered to teach him but he refused. When he asked me to do it, I agreed. But only because it was desperately important to him."

"Why would he ask you?" I said. "Why didn't he just talk

to me? What have *you* got to do with anything, Agnes?" My determination to say nothing hadn't lasted long.

She gave a sharp intake of breath, but I didn't care. That knot of resentment hadn't loosened.

"A good question," she said. "And you might not like the answer, Rob, but I'll give it to you anyway. I loved your grandfather and he loved me. There was even talk of marriage for a while there, but you know, in the end, it wasn't that important to either of us. He talked to me about you for hours and hours. I probably know more about you than I know about my own daughter, and certainly more than I know about *my* grandchild. Why? Because he loved you and you were what he wanted to talk about. Why did I listen? Because he loved me, I loved him, and whatever was important to him was important to me."

I didn't need to think about this right now. I shook my head.

"Your grandfather always worried about you," she continued. "About the panic attacks, about your shyness. In particular, the problems with your identity. He saw how, over the last couple of months, your confidence improved. He *loved* that, Rob. You probably didn't see many signs of it—Pat Fitzgerald never gave away many of his feelings—but he thought it was . . . miraculous. The challenges were his way of keeping you on the path toward self-respect. He saw your destination as happiness and wanted to guide you toward it. You probably think I've interfered, and I wouldn't blame you. Maybe you believe your grandfather interfered, but you must remember that all he wanted was your happiness. I can't expect your forgiveness, but he deserves it."

"Problems with my identity," I said. It was hard to force the words through my lips. "He talked to you about that?"

Agnes glanced down at a spot between her feet. The grass had worn away there and the dirt was as hard as truth.

"I told you," she said. "We talked about *everything*."

"I don't *have* problems with my identity," I said. "It's other people who have that."

Agnes held up both hands in surrender.

"I believe you, Rob," she said. "And I know it doesn't matter whether I believe it or not because it's none of my business. But your grandfather . . . well, he struggled with the . . . situation. You know that's true."

"Whatever," I said. "Let's leave that alone. Because you're right, Agnes. It really isn't any of your business." I held up my phone. "But let's talk about this, okay? Dramatic? Hey, I'll give you that. Let's scare Rob. Play around with messages from beyond the grave, is that it? A final challenge? But in the end, this is just cruelty. You know that, don't you?"

She rubbed her eyes. I looked at her directly for the first time and saw there were tracks of tears down her cheeks. I hadn't heard her crying. Suddenly I felt tired. Tired and guilty. It wasn't a good combination.

"Your grandfather wanted to give you one more

challenge," she said. "Not me, Rob. Your grandfather. I'm just the messenger, so please don't shoot me."

"And what did he want me to do?"

"You know." Agnes stood up. "You *know*, Rob. You talked about it, the two of you, and I know it was hard for him, that he had difficulty understanding. Your grandfather was from a generation that considered any display of feelings a weakness, particularly if you were male." She paused. "But he talked about it to you, because he loved you."

She picked up her handbag and slipped it onto her shoulder.

"The older I get, the less I understand," she said. "But this is the last message I've got to pass on and, frankly, I want to get it over with. Ignore it if you wish, or if you have to. Pat would never have wanted to make you do something you really couldn't face."

"Tell me," I said.

"'Stop hiding. Be proud of who you are.' That's it. The end. The final challenge." She held out her hand for me to shake. "I've got nothing else to say, Rob. I hope you'll forgive me, but I'm going home now to cry myself to sleep." She smiled as if to show she was joking. I looked at her hand and ignored it. We'd both loved him and that was a bond not easily broken.

I hugged Agnes and together we cried.

65

OVER THE FOLLOWING FEW WEEKS, I THOUGHT CAREFULLY about that conversation in my back garden.

I still went along to the Old Farts' Palace three times a week, mainly to take Trixie for a walk. Of course, I also spoke to Agnes, though she never mentioned the challenge again. We'd sometimes sit on the bench Grandad and I used to sit on in front of the dribbling fountain (it never got fixed, at least to my knowledge) and reminisce about Pop. Sometimes I'd cry, but mostly I'd laugh.

December arrived and with it the end of the school year. On the final day of school, there's a ritual as well established as our annual hammering at soccer by St. Martin's. This is the Christmas prizegiving assembly in front of the entire school, parents, and dignitaries. The local member of Parliament comes along, gives a speech, and sponsors a couple of prizes. It's a huge deal. And I know this sounds about as enjoyable as having your front teeth removed with rusty pliers and no anesthetic, but, believe it or not, it's a lot of fun.

There are three prizes for each grade, and the school pretends it's an Oscars ceremony. I know how lame that sounds, but it isn't. The event is hosted by the two school captains (newly elected juniors, one boy, one girl, since the seniors finish school before the end of the year), and they come dressed in a tuxedo and an evening gown (normally it's the boy wearing the tuxedo—normally). After a couple of musical performances by the school orchestra and a homegrown rock band (the winner of Milltown's Got Talent) accompanied by dance troupes, the ceremony gets under way. The hosts announce the name of the prize, and then there's a video clip of the entire grade, being idiots or playing sports. Often both at the same time. The hosts joke around and then a gold envelope is produced and opened to great fanfare and the winner's name announced.

The winners know who they are. The school tells them a good few weeks before the end of the year. This is partly to stop kids from getting themselves worked up, hoping they're going to win and then being desperately disappointed. It's also partly to ensure that the winners and their families turn up (the local newspaper always does a story on it, provided the reporter remembers to get out of bed).

Often the winner hams it up when his or her name is announced. They stand, openmouthed in mock shock, and stumble toward the stage, shaking hands with random people from the audience. Then they're allowed to give a short speech, most of the time something like, *I'd like to thank my parents, my theatrical agent, and Miss Cunningham for shouting at me all year.* The drama students really get into it, sobbing realistically and impersonating actors who've made idiots of themselves at the real Oscars. In fact, it's because of the drama students that a time limit was introduced by the school a few years back. Now the winners have two minutes, though most are happy just to mumble "Thanks" and get off the stage.

I'd already been told I was a prizewinner. Sports Personality of Eighth Grade, of all things.

I couldn't help but think this was a sign.

66

I SAT NEXT TO MY PARENTS IN MY DESIGNATED SEAT about ten rows from the stage. This was so that when my name was called I'd have a distance to walk, thus giving me the opportunity to ham it up if I chose.

I wasn't going to ham it up.

The other award winners were scattered throughout the audience, but the drama department (who were responsible for organizing the whole evening) knew exactly where everyone was. When your name was called, a spotlight picked you out and followed your progress to the steps at the side of the stage.

I told you it was a big deal.

The rock band played against a backdrop of the Milltown's Got Talent video. I'd had no idea anyone was filming the show, but I guess I shouldn't have been surprised. Milltown has an enthusiastic film and video department as well as a lively drama department. Nonetheless, it was a shock to see excerpts of my Macbeth act mingled in with the other performances. A shock, but also . . . nice. There was no sound, of course, since the band was playing, but I thought I looked professional. Mind you, the drama department hadn't exactly been hammering my metaphorical door down since the show.

The band finished, the audience shook their heads to get rid of the ringing, and the ceremony began.

It starts with the youngest members of the school and works up to the juniors. This is fair and also practical. The juniors tend to say little; the entertainment usually comes from the seniors and their sometimes funny and sometimes annoying self-confidence. It took no time to get through seventh grade, and then it was my year's turn.

The first prize was for Greatest Academic Performance of Eighth Grade. The hosts tried to make a big deal of it, but they didn't try too hard. Those of us toward the bottom of the school pile aren't of much interest to anyone, apparently. There was a backdrop of various scenes in classrooms—kids gazing into microscopes, raising their hands as a teacher asked a question, heads bent over books, rummaging around the library shelves—you get the idea.

"And the winner is . . ." The male school captain made a big deal of fumbling with the envelope while a drum roll played in the background. He finally pulled a card free. "Amit Singh," he shouted. There was wild applause and a spotlight hit the rows to my right. Everyone craned their necks to see.

A very small boy got to his feet and walked toward the stage, head down. It was obvious to everyone he was going to stutter a terrified "Thanks" before scuttling back to safety. The female school captain took a trophy from the table behind her and prepared to hand it to Amit. The boy stumbled getting up the steps but recovered in time. He took the trophy, which was almost as big as him, and approached the podium. The audience could barely see him over it, and the male captain had to bend the microphone down toward his mouth.

"Thanks," Amit mumbled. It was kinda weird, like a disembodied voice echoing around the hall.

He took a step away and then, obviously remembering something, returned. "Thank you, teachers of Milltown," he said. "I love you all."

Everybody roared with laughter. You could feel a tide of affection rolling toward Amit as he made his way down the steps and back to his family. I watched his mum and dad. Pride radiated from them and I was almost blinded by it.

This was going to be a hard act to follow. But follow it I must, because I was next.

"The following award is for Sports Personality of Eighth Grade," said the female school captain. They were obviously taking turns. Mum squeezed my hand, but I felt calm. Now that the moment was upon me, I was okay with it. "There have been many examples of good sports personalities in eighth grade this year," she continued, "and here is a reminder of some of them."

The stage darkened and the huge screen behind the presenters lit up once more. Basketball action, cross-country running, some halfhearted rugby tackles. And, mixed in with all of it, the soccer game against St. Martin's. In particular, me, Rob Fitzgerald, making save after save after save. I could tell by the way Mum squeezed my hand harder that she was impressed, maybe even startled, by what she saw. What was even more remarkable were the cheers and shouts that greeted my performance.

Finally, the video ended.

"And the winner is . . ." The school captain tore open the envelope and took out the card. "Well, this is a surprise," she said. "Who'd believe it? The winner is . . . Rob Fitzgerald."

I stood and found myself in a bubble of blinding light.

I'd pretty much got my panic attacks under control, but there's something strange about walking in a spotlight pool onto a stage in front of hundreds of strangers. I tried to focus. *One step at a time*, I told myself. *Literally. Get to the steps at the side of the stage. Climb the steps and don't fall down. Take the trophy from the school captain. Don't drop it. Move to the lectern. Speak. Simple.*

But it all took so long . . .

And yet it took no time at all. Suddenly I had the trophy in my hand and I stepped up to the lectern. What I hadn't been expecting was the weight of silence as I stood there. My shoulders bowed under it.

I cleared my throat and the short explosion through the

microphone made me jump. Somewhere in the audience someone sniggered.

"Thanks," I said. The silence settled once more and sweat gathered on my forehead. "My name is Rob Fitzgerald," I continued. "That's me. Rob. I'm a boy." This time there was a smatter of laughter. The spotlight meant I couldn't see much of the audience—just a couple of rows at the front. There were a few puzzled expressions in those rows but also some smiles that felt like encouragement. In my peripheral vision I saw the school captain step forward as if to move me on, and I knew time was running out.

And then I saw Daniel Smith. He sat in the second row, to my left, and there was a half smile on his face. Suddenly my head cleared and I spoke directly to him. "I'm a boy," I repeated. "But I was born in the wrong body. Simple as that. I don't know how many kids in this school knew I'm trans. If it was ever a secret, I guess it isn't anymore. So, yeah. I'm Rob Fitzgerald, an eighth-grade boy in Milltown High School. That's all. Thanks."

There was some applause as I made my way back to my seat but it died quickly. I walked through silence and was thrilled that I didn't trip up once.

67

ALMOST AS SOON AS WE GOT HOME, DAD WENT TO THE
pub to watch football with his mates.

"What do you say to some takeout, Rob?" Mum asked
when the noise of Dad's car had faded into the night.

"How about beans on toast?" I replied. Mum smiled. We
used to love sitting in front of the television, a plate of beans
on toast on our laps, solving all the problems of the world.
Or at least the problems in whatever soap opera we happened to be watching. It was pretty much a ritual when I
was in elementary school, and I missed it.

"It's a massively complicated dish," she said, "but it's
not every day you're awarded Sports Personality of Eighth
Grade, Rob, so I'm prepared to work my culinary magic.
Stick some bread into the toaster, would you?"

This time there was no soap opera. We sat in the front
room, each on our own sofa, the television dark, and ate

our beans. Mum had a glass of white wine at her feet, while I had Trixie at mine, drooling and never taking her eyes off my plate. Yes, Mum and Dad had finally allowed me to keep her. According to Mum, they'd watched to see if I still went to walk her after Grandad died. Once they were convinced this was a love affair to stand the test of time, they bought a dog bed, a doghouse, and a supply of balanced dog food especially formulated for fluffy bundles of rubbish. I was happy. I think Trixie was happy as well, but it's difficult to tell, since she only stops yapping at everything when there's food around.

"You're not getting my beans," I told her. "That is begging, and anyway you'll fart all night."

Trixie wasn't impressed with this line of reasoning. She never lost focus, even when a particularly long and viscous trail of drool made a puddle at her feet.

"Gross," I said.

"That was a surprise tonight, Rob," said Mum. I knew this was a conversation we were going to have once Dad had left. It was fair enough, too. I hadn't given them any warning, mainly because I think Dad might not have come along and that would've been heartbreaking.

"Sorry, Mum," I said.

"No need to apologize," she replied. "I think it was brave." Mum lifted a forkful of beans to her lips, and one slid off down her cleavage. "Damn it," she said. "I hate it when that happens."

I laughed. It had happened nearly every time in the past and it always made me laugh. I went to get paper towels while Mum burrowed down her top in search of the escapee.

"It's just that . . . I dunno. I thought this was something you didn't feel the need to advertise to the world. You've said that in the past." She found the bean and lifted it triumphantly before placing it on the paper towel. I took it to the trash can for a decent, if unceremonious, burial.

Then I explained about Grandad and the text message challenges, Agnes's part in them (I didn't say anything about their love for each other—that wasn't my story to tell), and how what happened at the awards ceremony was not so much because *I* felt the need, but because it was the last challenge and obviously important to Grandad.

"So you did it for him?"

"Yes," I said. "In part. But it wasn't a . . . gesture. Those challenges *have* helped, Mum. I used to be such a scared little mouse."

"You're still a mouse."

"Yeah, but not quite as little and not quite as scared."

"Obviously. Nonetheless, it took guts to say all of that in front of so many people."

I folded my legs beneath me and hugged a cushion to my chest.

"I'd thought about it really carefully," I said. "I don't know how many kids at Milltown knew I'm trans—they *all* know now, of course—but some obviously did. Anyway, I thought that if I was going to do it, then it was important to also stress my identity. This is where I came from, but Rob is who I am."

Mum took another sip of wine and then burst out laughing. Unfortunately, this propelled a stream of wine from her nose and I had to rush over with yet more paper towels. Even when she'd regained control, tears of laughter still ran down her cheeks. Or it might have been wine.

"That is so gross," I said. "I thought Trixie was gross, but you've outdone her."

"Sorry," said Mum. She blew her nose long and hard. "I just had the worst thought."

I waved an encouraging hand.

"Your grandfather *loved* to interfere and you'd think that death might have slowed him down. But no. That silly old bastard is still interfering from beyond the grave."

I smiled. It was true.

And it was also true that he would've loved to hear Mum say that.

I got the text in bed at ten thirty.

Uve got the drama stuff sorted rob
give u that

I hadn't been able to sleep anyway, so I turned on my bedside lamp and thought about my reply.

I aim to please, Andrew. Any clue as to the
general reaction from the public?

Wtf plus bit more wtf

You're a wordsmith.

I no

Have you even heard of punctuation?

Only rumors

Will everyone hate me?

**They did b4 so no change how u
feeling**

Is this you being considerate about my
feelings, Andrew?

No will deny it to death just asking

I feel fine. Even if there's bound to be a few
more kids wanting to beat me up.

Good job im ur mate then

Yes, but not just for that reason.

Go away freak

Night night.

Dad came in well after midnight. Judging by the noise he made getting his keys into the lock, he'd had a bit too much to drink. When I went to my bedroom window and parted the curtains, I was relieved to see he hadn't driven home.

68

THE ONE ADVANTAGE TO DROPPING A BOMBSHELL AT the end of the school year is that you don't have to face the consequences until the *following* year.

I was pleased by that nearly six weeks' break.

Christmas was fun once I accepted I wasn't going to find Grandad sitting in front of the television after lunch, snoring and breaking wind. Andrew wasn't around either because his family goes to Queensland every year to spend time with relatives, but he texted me often, mainly, I suspect, to annoy me with his spelling and punctuation. I have this sneaking feeling that when he texts anyone else, he writes normal stuff. But with me, he's getting worse. I mean, *meri krissmuss*? Come on, Andrew. That's just desperate.

So we stayed at home, though on Boxing Day we drove to the Old Farts' Palace to take some presents and a huge bowl of trifle that is Mum's specialty. Agnes gave me a big hug and whispered in my ear: "So what do you think, Rob? Who's going to die next? My money's on Alf over there."

I can't tell you how much I loved that.

Most of the time I took Trixie for long, rambling walks or spent hours in my bedroom, writing. Ninth grade was a scary prospect when I thought about it, so I tried not to think about it. The writing helped. So did Trixie.

I'd avoided the park where Destry walked her dog, possibly because I wasn't sure how she'd react the next time she saw me. But then I remembered Pop's last challenge. *Stop hiding. Be proud of who you are.* What was the point of that whole prizegiving stunt if I tried to avoid people?

So I found myself on a bench in the park at about two thirty on a Monday afternoon. It was a very hot day and the weather had even calmed Trixie down a little; she'd walked at my side like a proper dog rather than something demented or possibly demonic. Then again, there weren't many people or dogs around, so that helped. In this kind of weather, the temptation was to stay at home or find an ocean to swim in. I would like it placed on record that I did *not* go to the park at the time when Destry normally walked her hound.

It didn't matter, because I'd only sat there for ten minutes when she turned a corner, attached to something that could have doubled for Rudolph in an emergency, if you were prepared to overlook the absence of a red nose. And antlers.

One minute later, Destry was sitting at my side, the dog perched next to her like a muscly mountain. Trixie tried a steely gaze, a small yelp, and then thought better of it and fell asleep.

"Merry Christmas, Rob," said Destry.

"You too," I replied. "What did the big fat guy in red bring you?"

Quite a bit, it turned out. We exchanged tales of Christmas gifts, dinners, and embarrassing family encounters. For all that, I couldn't help but think we were avoiding the one subject on our minds. Or at least the one subject on *my* mind.

"I'm so sorry about your grandfather," she said. Had I really not spoken to her since Pop's death? Apparently not. "He seemed like a real . . . character."

"'Character' is one way of putting it," I said. "Some people would've put it another way."

"Was it right what he said?"

"About what?"

"That you were in love with me?"

Ah. Good old Grandad. Little more than a bag of ashes but still capable of embarrassing me. I thought. A good number of possible replies ran through my head.

"Yes," I said.

"And do you *still* love me?"

This was trickier. *I'm thirteen years old and this is the first time I've been in love*, I thought. *I've got nothing else to compare it to. Maybe it feels like love but it's actually a rare form of indigestion. Anyway, my feelings have changed. Or have they? Is it simply that so many things have happened that I can't maintain that level of intensity toward her?* Hell. I had no idea.

"Maybe," I said.

We sat in silence for a minute or two.

"Loved the prizegiving ceremony," she said finally. "You stole the show."

"Thanks," I said. There was another pause. "Did you know I was trans before that?" I added. I had to ask, even though I had no idea if the answer was going to be of the slightest importance.

"Oh, yes," she said. "It wasn't a closely guarded secret, you know. In any school, if one kid knows, everyone knows. That's just the way it is."

I nodded. I should have thought about that, because it's so obviously true. Gossip makes the school world go around. I lifted up my head to say just this, but the words never arrived.

Destry stopped them. By kissing me.

69

IT WAS A LONG KISS, MY FIRST ONE. AND SWEET.

When she was done (I didn't take much of an active role in the process, other than shutting my eyes and keeping my mouth open and my brain from overheating), Destry took my hand in hers, though I noticed she avoided eye contact. I kept quiet because I had no idea what to say.

"I don't want you to get the wrong impression, Rob," she said finally.

My brain wasn't at its finest, it has to be said, but I had some difficulty processing this. She'd just kissed me. How could any impression I got be wrong?

"I have a boyfriend," she continued, "and I'm happy with him." It occurred to me that if she was that happy, she wouldn't be kissing someone else, but who am I to make judgments about romance? I'm no expert, that's for sure. So I kept silent.

"But I've wanted to do that for a long time."

"Okay," I said. What else could I say?

She got to her feet and her dog lumbered to his. I stood as well. Call me old-fashioned. Trixie snored.

"Hey," she said, as if an amusing thought had just struck her. "If I *had* been your girlfriend, would that have made you gay?"

It had taken me virtually no time to fall in love with Destry Camberwick. I remembered her entrance into my classroom vividly. The world had stopped turning on its axis and her beauty had been a punch in the gut. It wasn't a rare form of indigestion. It had been love, or at least a variation of it. What I hadn't realized was how it was possible to fall instantly *out* of love. I did now. That kiss had been sweet and unexpected and wonderful. Now it felt . . . tainted.

"We kissed," I said. "That makes me straight. What do you think it makes you, Destry?"

There was hurt in her eyes and I knew we'd almost certainly never speak again. As I watched her leave the park, I couldn't find it in myself to care.

I went home and told Mum I was going to Brisbane next July with the state under-sixteen soccer team.

"That's great," she said. "But what about panic attacks, public toilets, and problems around dressing rooms?"

"No idea," I said. "I guess if they really want me in that squad, they'll have to sort that stuff out for me."

70

"YOU MADE ME A CHARACTER IN YOUR BOOK," SAID
Ms. Pritchett. "That's so sweet, Rob."

My monthly meeting, a twenty-five-minute bus ride from
our house. Summer's heat was building and the bus had been
stuffy, the passengers quiet and grumpy. I don't know how I
could tell the mood when no one was saying anything, but
I knew. I felt a bit grumpy myself. The forecast was over a
hundred degrees for the next few days. God help us all. Ms.
P's office is ten minutes' walk from the bus terminal, so I was
irritable *and* sweaty when I arrived. Not for the first time I
wondered why I bother with this every four weeks, and not
for the first time I came up with the answer. There's something pleasant about routine and there's also something lib-
erating about talking to someone for an hour, knowing you
don't have to make any pretenses because no judgments are
being made. Plus, her office has air conditioning . . .

It wasn't like that at the start, of course (she'd *always* had air conditioning, though), but Ms. Pritchett had gained my trust over the years and hadn't let me down. That was why I'd given her that whopping sheaf of papers she called my "book"—I got a little shiver when she said that, I don't mind admitting—because I knew she'd read it, for one thing, and there'd be nothing in there she didn't already know quite a bit about.

"I thought you'd get a kick out of it," I replied.

Ms. Pritchett picked up that fat pile of paper from her desk and started flicking through it. I looked around the office to see if anything was different—it's a little game I play—but the same framed certificates were on the walls, the same photograph of her daughter on the desk, positioned at an angle so she could see it and anyone sitting on my side of the desk could as well. I liked that. It made me feel just a tiny bit included in her life while I included her in mine.

"It's terrific, you know," she said. "You should get it published."

"Oh, no," I said, in a pathetic attempt at modesty. *Oh, YES!* I screamed inside my head.

"It's very imaginative."

"English teachers have remarked upon this before," I said. "Apparently it's discussed enthusiastically in staff rooms, which only proves they need to get out more . . ." I stopped, while my brain delivered the results from its processing of her words. "Hang on," I continued. "What do you mean by that?"

Ms. Pritchett put the sheaf back down on the desk. A small puff of dust lingered in a sunbeam from the window behind her, motes dancing. She leaned back in her chair and made her fingers form a steeple.

"I mean, you've taken a couple of . . . liberties with the truth."

I pointed at the papers. "Ninety-nine percent of that is pure fact," I said. I think there was indignation in my voice. I hope so, because I felt it.

"I'm not a teacher at your school, Rob."

I waved a hand. "Oh, come on. That character plays only a small part in the story and I just put it in for a bit of fun. Like I said, I thought you'd *like* to be in it."

"I could easily have been. We've been meeting for . . . what, four years now, Rob? Yet there's not one mention of that in this book."

"Our meetings are not very exciting, Ms. Pritchett," I said. "Sorry to break it to you." I knew I was being snotty, but she was dissing my writing. Not in an obvious way, I admit, but that's how I felt.

"That's true," she said. I was annoyed that her tone of voice betrayed no emotional reaction to my comment, especially since that was what I'd been aiming for. "But I think it's interesting your fictional teacher is the one protecting you from Daniel Smith."

"It's not *interesting*," I said. "It's meant to be funny."

She ignored me.

"A teacher with superpowers, always there to protect you."

I snorted. "Come on, Ms. P. I mean, jeez. Ever heard of humor? Hello?"

She ignored me again. "That would have been useful in the real world, wouldn't it, Rob? Because, as you've told me on many occasions, there *was* no one to protect you at school, apart from Andrew, and he couldn't be there all the time." I tried to interrupt, but she was having none of it. "And a good few others who gave you grief at school appear to have disappeared from your narrative. All lumped together in the one character of Daniel Smith."

"There weren't *that* many others . . ."

"Should I review my notes, Rob?"

I said nothing and tried to regulate my breathing. I know what I wanted to say—that not one of those certificates on the wall said qualified psychiatrist. But that wasn't going to work. Ms. Pritchett had stuff she wanted to get off her chest, and nothing I could do, short of leaving, would stop it. *It's kinda ironic*, I thought. *I'm normally the one talking and she's the one listening.* Our roles appeared to have reversed, and perhaps that would be . . . interesting.

"What else is untrue in my story?" I asked when I'd calmed down a bit. "Come on. You talk and I'll listen."

She gave a half smile at that.

"Okay," she said. "Here's what I think. I think you have

told your story with typical humor and decency, but sacrificed things in order to present an idealized version of your world. You're right. The Miss Pritchett character is a small example. But what about your grandfather? The way you tell it, he never had any significant problems with you being trans, but that's not true." She got up from her chair and stood at the window, her back to me. It would be nice to say she looked out on a cityscape or a park with joggers, and mums and dads pushing prams. But the only view was of a discolored brick wall and a potholed section of car park. "Of course, the most severe . . . *reworking* of reality is with your portrayal of your father. In the narrative he's always understanding and supportive. True, there were hints right at the end—the section about the school prizegiving is the best example—that he wasn't comfortable with your gender identity, but generally you give the impression of a harmonious home life filled with unqualified love and support."

She turned to face me. The beam of sunlight had gone now—I had no idea how it had intruded in the first place, given the outlook from the office window. Maybe it had been a reflection from a car windshield. "I'm not being critical, Rob. Honestly, I love your book and you made me cry. But I also have a professional responsibility and I worry you're trying to create the world you'd *like* to exist, rather than facing up to the one you're stuck with. Remember, I've accompanied you for at least a part of your journey and I *know* the massive obstacles you've had to overcome. Are still overcoming."

I sat in my chair for a long time, saying nothing. It was important to frame my response carefully and rationally, especially since emotions were bubbling up and threatening to overwhelm. Sometimes, these days, just the mention of Grandad's name can do that. But I was wounded. So I tried to see things from Ms. Pritchett's point of view, and that calmed me. I could see why some stuff in my book would worry her. And there was another irony. We had discussed many times how my ability—my *determination*, Ms. P said—to always see the other person's point of view was a good thing and a bad thing. She hinted that my empathy sometimes made me want to forgive the unforgivable. I thought it made me a nice person.

Ms. Pritchett gave me a wad of tissues. I hadn't even realized I was crying. So I snorted and sniffed and was generally disgusting for a few minutes. But it helped. My voice trembled only slightly when I spoke.

"Thanks," I said. I dropped a large, wet bundle of tissues into the bin and gave one last revolting sniff. "I'll try to explain. First of all, the other kids and Daniel Smith. I told you about threats at school because . . . well, obviously they hurt. But I also said, many times, that this wasn't the whole story." I brushed a wayward strand of hair behind my ear. "Maybe you think Milltown High is full of prejudiced bullies, but it isn't. It *really* isn't. Yeah, some kids gave me grief, as you put it, but most didn't. They *did* accept me. They *were* supportive." I pointed at the photograph on the desk. "You've got a daughter about my age, Ms. P. I don't know if she talks to you much. I can't imagine you do to her what you do to me." She smiled at that, but said nothing. "Kids of our age, I think, are tolerant in ways older generations aren't. Most kids simply don't care. Provided you don't hurt anyone, they're cool with the color of your skin, your sexuality, your size, or the way you dress." Ms. Pritchett put a finger to her lips as if considering the point, so I carried on. "Yeah, some kids care about *all* those things—the bullies, the nasties, the unpleasant pieces of work. But, trust me, they're the minority and they'd have a go at *anyone* they thought was different. Ask your daughter. I think she'd agree."

Ms. Pritchett took her seat again. It was obvious she'd resumed listening mode, because there was silence for ten or fifteen seconds and she seemed in no hurry to break it.

"Grandad," I said finally. "Ah, Grandad." I took another tissue because it's best to be prepared. I pointed at the manuscript. "Everything in there about Pop is true. *Everything*. Sure, he had difficulty understanding when I first told him, maybe three years ago, but who wouldn't? I remember he said to me, 'But, Roberta, why would you *want* to be a boy? Boys grow up to be men, and men are blankety idiots. It's men who've caused all the blankety wars in history. It's men who blankety hurt women. If I could, I'd be a woman, because men are the blankety scum of the earth.'" I rubbed at my nose with the tissue. The way this hour was going, I'd be doing a good impersonation of Rudolph by the end. Unfortunately, I'd left my festive antlers at home.

"So what did you say to that?" I must have been quiet for longer than I thought, lost in memories, because Ms. P doesn't normally have to jog me.

"I said, 'That's the point, Grandad. *If I could.* But you can't be a woman and neither can I. It's not a question of me *wanting* to be a boy. There's no choice involved. A boy is who I am.'"

"Did he understand?"

"Not really. Not fully. But you know what's more important, Ms. P? He tried. He tried so hard. And he accepted me, loved me, for who and what I am." I placed my hand on the pile of paper. "*That's* what I hope is in here."

She nodded. "And your father?"

"Oh, Dad." I laughed. "He was *so* embarrassed that night of the awards ceremony. Didn't speak to me for four days, came home that night rotten drunk. But before that he was normally okay—provided the subject of me being trans never came up or, God forbid, was ever discussed. Mum called him the fat ostrich. The golfing ostrich with his head in a bunker, showing his butt to the world."

Ms. Pritchett smiled. "But not openly supportive."

"Oh, Ms. P," I said. "You want everyone to be perfect."

"Sometimes I think I'd like you to act like a

thirteen-year-old. You're way too mature for a kid of your age."

"No pleasing some people, poopy-face," I replied.

"Do you think trans people grow up quicker?" she asked. There was genuine curiosity there.

I gave it thought because it had never occurred to me before.

"Maybe," I said finally. "We have to *deal* with things others don't. As you said, I've struggled to get to where I am now. Plenty of pain and suffering that most people can't even think about. And probably more to come." I pointed at her. "But you'd probably know better than I do. You're the authority. What do you think?"

"I think I'm not trans."

I laughed at that. "Okay," I said. "Earlier you thought my book was . . . what were your words? An idealized world. Something about me writing a world I *wanted* to exist, but that didn't, not really. That's not true, Ms. Pritchett. It does exist. I think people are good and kind. Generally. Sure, there're bad people out there. Whoopy doo. But I didn't want to write about bad people, partly because that's my choice, partly because they're on the wrong side of human history, but mainly because I feel good about myself. I feel *normal*. Perhaps that will change, but at the moment, I feel normal."

We gazed at each other for a few moments. Then Ms. Pritchett snatched a tissue from the dispenser and dabbed at her eyes.

"Get the hell out of here, Rob," she said. "You've over-stayed your hour and your welcome." But she smiled as she said it.

The walk back to the bus was hard work, especially since the heat was trying to suck the life out of me. Anyone who could, stayed in air-conditioned cars or buildings. We pedestrians shuffled along like the walking dead.

I had my earbuds in, my phone tucked into my jeans pocket. Sweat trickled down my forehead.

But I felt good, walking to the beat of a song only I could hear.

ACKNOWLEDGMENTS

I want to sincerely thank all who talked to me about the experience of being transgender. In particular, I much appreciate the frank and open responses of Stephanie Spillett, a former student of mine, who spent considerable time answering my, at times, very personal questions about gender dysphoria and her experiences in primary and senior schools. Ira Racines, another former student and now a prominent member of the LGBTQI+ community in Darwin, Australia, who works with trans kids from time to time, read the manuscript and made many constructive comments, guiding both my thinking and my writing. I also had an illuminating conversation with Daniel Alderman, who works closely with trans people in Darwin, and he made many perceptive comments about the portrayal of transgender people. Lucy Gunner, a leading Pride organizer in the Northern Territory, read the manuscript twice, which is above and beyond the call of duty. Some of the dialogue in this book was unashamedly stolen from her, and I'm grateful for her guidance, good humor, and intelligence. Thanks also to good friend and excellent English teacher Cathy Hood for reading the final copy and offering valuable insight.

It goes without saying that any errors or clumsiness or lack of sensitivity that may remain within these pages are my responsibility only.

Scot Gardner, author extraordinaire and good friend, read the first draft of *A Song Only I Can Hear* and made his normal perceptive and constructive remarks. Another fabulous author, Michael Gerard Bauer, very kindly read the (nearly) final version and was generous enough to speak highly of it. Thanks to both for the way they have always supported my writing and for being genuinely thrilled when I have achieved anything in the way of success. My publisher, Jodie Webster, has been with me from the start of my writing career, and her belief in me has been unwavering. Readers often have little idea of the importance of an editor in shaping a book, making it the very best it can be, and the huge amount of time spent in doing so. My editor, Kate Whitfield, has edited this book with her customary care and sensitivity, and I thank her for all her hard work. Thanks too to Carey Schroeter and Angela Namoi, who have taken my books into the international market.

Although the epigraph in the opening pages is commonly attributed to Oscar Wilde, I'm aware that this attribution is doubtful. But whoever said it, the spirit of the words felt true to Wilde, and he, in turn, feels true to the spirit of this book.

Finally, my family has been exceptionally supportive, as always. Thanks to Lauren, Brendan, and more distant family members who've egged me on from afar.

As for my wife, Nita, well, not only does she give me the time and the encouragement to write, but she is also my first reader, someone whose judgment I trust and have always trusted. I don't think I could write without her support and belief. And, of course, it helps that she sings a song only I can hear.